T0078165

Haley's Star

Book Three of the Shooting Star Series

Lesley Esposito

authorHOUSE®

AuthorHouse™
1663 Liberty Drive
Bloomington, IN 47403
www.authorhouse.com
Phone: 1 (800) 839-8640

Published by AuthorHouse 02/01/2017

ISBN: 978-1-5246-5878-6 (sc)
ISBN: 978-1-5246-5877-9 (e)

Library of Congress Control Number: 2017900226

Print information available on the last page.

Print information available on the last page.

Chapter 1

Allie sighed as she looked out her apartment window. There was nothing wrong in particular. In fact she was thrilled that she had finally made it to New York City. She had spent years working her way up in class of hotels as assistant manager. After spending her summer working in a beach resort city she had finally landed a job in a new hotel as the weekend night manager. She still had plans of one day becoming the general manager but she at least made it to the city of her dreams.

It was the weather that was getting her down. Her brother was coming to town and it was too wet and blustery to do anything outside. Truly, she knew her brother was really visiting his girlfriend, also a resident of the city, but she was grateful for the few hours they would be together. It was going to be a nice distraction.

She had only been there for a few weeks and she knew she had to be more patient. Allie knew a few people but no one close by. It had been harder than she thought to meet people and make friends. She had imagined herself going to clubs, galleries, fundraisers. While she did not expect to be high society she was more than ready to experience everything the city had to offer.

And because she worked weekends it was doubly hard to meet people. She knew there were happenings every night in the city, trying to figure out where to start was the hard part. She did not want to venture out by herself to any bars or clubs not knowing the reputation of random places. She was also not ready to resort to online services. Another issue was the residents of her building were mostly older couples. She had no problem with couple friends but they did not have quite the same going out mindset. She would have to join a club or a group to meet some people. She planned to pick up some local papers on her excursions. Allie stepped away from the window sipping the last of her coffee. Without really looking she put the mug on the counter before heading to the bathroom to shower. Just as she was about to step onto the cool tiles, which did not take a long since she lived in a studio apartment, she heard the crash of ceramic shattering on the kitchen floor. She quickly turned in confusion, it seemed odd the cup had just fallen. She could not say for sure that she had placed the mug squarely on the counter. She sighed, shrugged her shoulders and turned back to clean up the pieces.

An hour later she was walking to meet her brother. His girlfriend only lived a few blocks away. Alex had driven up from his school in Williamsburg for the weekend. Allie wanted to spend every minute she could with him so they agreed to meet there before they headed downtown. She wrapped her overcoat around her a little tighter as the rain started coming down harder and sideways. She walked faster as she dodged a turning car crossing the normally quiet intersection. She reached the entrance and made a quick dash inside the lobby. Her brother was already waiting for her since his girlfriend was still at work.

"Alex," she ran over and gave her brother a big wet hug.

"Hey sis," he greeted her back while pushing her away. "You know there is such a thing as an umbrella."

"It's just a little water," she said while punching him lightly on the shoulder. "I am so glad you are here. I know you are mostly here to see Katie but I am glad we get to hang out for a little while."

"Hey I came to see you also."

"Well, I am glad. And since it is raining I figured we would just head downtown to the Columbus Circle Mall; have some lunch, do some window shopping. Sound okay? I will leave the sightseeing stuff to Katie."

"Anything is fine, better than sitting around by myself."

"We are about two blocks from the subway, we can make a quick break for it," Allie peered outside and it was still raining pretty heavily. She did not want to spend the extra on a cab and she only had a few hours with her brother so she wanted to head out.

"I'm getting you an umbrella for Christmas," her brother responded with a grin. Thirty minutes later they walked up to street level, the skies were a touch brighter with just a light drizzle falling. Still too wet to stroll through Central Park they headed to the large glass enclosed mall. They entered through glass doors into an enormous lobby lined with four stories of windows. The surrounding balconies from each floor showcased glass fronted stores with the latest in fashions.

Allie stood giddy with excitement. Not exactly Fifth Avenue but it would do. Besides she did not quite have the funds for the higher priced shopping. When her brother caught her attention she remembered she was there to spend time with him.

"Careful you might start to drool," he teased her noticing the glimmer in her eyes as they scanned around. She always had a knack for fashion even with their limited means growing up.

"Sorry," she replied instinctively touching the side of her lips. "Shall we find a restaurant?"

They located the directory and settle on pub fare. Once the drinks and food were ordered they caught up with each other.

"How is school going?" Allie asked Alex who was a graduate student studying historic architecture.

"Good, there is a lot happening in Rome right now that we are keeping up with. Every time renovations are started or a new building breaks ground artifacts are dug up. The construction work has to stop so the historical society can come in and assess the finds."

"Maybe you will get to take a trip there?"

"I don't know, I think I am going to stay with post civil war building renovations." Alex looked around avoiding eye contact with his sister.

"Oh I see, it's pretty serious with Katie? Plan on moving here after school?"

"Maybe, I just don't want you to think that would be my only reason, this is a great city. Besides you made the move here."

"Hey, I am not judging, as long as you are happy." Alex and Katie had not known each other very long and only managed a long distance relationship with a few short visits. Still they seemed happy together and were willing to wait through Alex's last year of school. "Besides, I would love to have you here." With limited family Allie and her brother maintained a close relationship and had just spent the summer together in the same house.

"I have been talking to Ben, he gave me a few contacts for when I graduate. Did you know he is selling his apartment and planning to move south to be with Emma?" Alex was excited thinking he may know something his sister did not.

Allie was in fact shocked, "really? Does Emma know about this?" Emma was her last roommate, actually homeowner of the house she lived in for the past year. They had known each other in college and reconnected when they both moved south. Emma had met Ben during the summer and like her brother was managing a long distance relationship.

"No. He is surprising her, he has been planning it since the summer. And you can't tell her."

Allie made a pouty face with that. "That is not fair. I am not so sure she will like that sprung on her."

"Please don't say anything. In any case he is aware that she may say no but he plans on moving to the area, get his own place if he has to."

"Well I hope she says yes, he is a good guy and she deserves him." Allie reflected on the fact that the people closest to her were building long term relationships. She had made a decision long ago to avoid that. She did not want to lose sight of her goal to live in New York. She had seen too many of her college friends change their plans in life because of boyfriends. She did not want to ever have to make that choice. Now that she was where she wanted to be she was ready to be open to relationships. The city was full of possibilities, she just needed to figure out how to take advantage of them.

Alex finally broke through her thoughts when he asked her how she was enjoying living in the city. She put on her best smile and said, "it's great!"

Her brother knew better though, "I am sure it is but how are you really doing?"

She never kept anything from her brother and even though he did not often have answers or advice she could speak freely to him. "I do like it here, I am just antsy. I need to meet people and go places and do things. I only know four people here. Ben is leaving so that makes three. Jason and Molly are married and Katie is wrapped up with you and her work. Also the apartment is great, I will always be appreciative that Molly is letting me use it. It's just far from everything. I am ready to be in the center of everything, be a part of the social scene."

Alex was hiding his amusement, "you have been here for what, three weeks? You need to give it some time."

"I know, I feel like I am that actor expecting to jump into the starring role on Broadway because I am fabulous and everyone should know that." Of course she could not sing or dance but she was good at her job and did plan on excelling there.

"Sis, you are fabulous." And practically reading her mind he asked, "how is your job?"

Allie did manage a genuine smile this time, "it is exciting being there from the opening. There have been a few kinks to work out, otherwise it is going well."

"Maybe you can hook up with some coworkers there and go out with them?"

"I am still getting to know the staff and figuring out who I could do that with. Working weekend nights does not help. Still this is the city that never sleeps so I am hopeful."

They wrapped up their meal talking about their childhood, where they were at the moment and life in general. They had a little more time to spend together so they decided to wander around the mall. They noticed a crowd of people and decided to investigate. There was a model search going on. They saw an elevated judges table with a cat walk running perpendicular it. There was a crowd of people in front of the stage, neither one of the siblings had a whole lot of interest in what was going on but it would at least make for some great people watching. They managed to find a bench that was just behind and to the side of the judges so they could catch a glimpse of each contestant as well as the reaction of the judges.

"I did not think mall model searches still existed," Alex commented.

Allie shrugged, "maybe the pool of beautiful people is diminishing."

"I doubt that," Alex said with a look of skepticism.

They sat watching for a while rating each girl on a scale of one to ten. Most were five or sixes in their opinion with a few at the top of the scale. Alex leaned over, "you could beat out most of these girls. You're tall enough, and pretty cute, for a sister that is."

Allie stood up and walked up and down in front of Alex pretending to be on a runway. She exaggerated each step lifting her feet higher then was natural. At the end of her run she put her hands on her hips shifting her weight from side to side while pursing her lips together. When she looked to the side to see Alex's reaction he was looking past her. She turned to see one of the judges standing up smiling at her with a crooked grin softly clapping his hands. She gave him a second look noting not so much as amusement to his dark eyes but more of a curiosity. He was tall and lean, well dressed in a dark casual manner. He had a wide swath of dark medium length hair with each side shaved off. Allie wondered if he was a model himself. She gave the man a slight nod and a curtsy. He responded with his own nod. He bent down to pick up some papers that had fallen to the floor without taking his eyes off her. Once the papers were back in their proper place he turned his focus back on the contest.

Allie quickly turned and sat next to her brother. She grinned, "what do you think, he's pretty cute."

Alex pretended to assess the situation, "well he is not really my type. I do think you should make a few more passes. Make him smile again."

Allie watched cute guy for a few more minutes. She watched his reaction as each girl stepped up to be judged and scrutinized. She was trying to figure out his expression. He did not seem bored or uninterested, he also did not seem too excited either. Perhaps it was a look of frustration or disappointment. Her brother was right though, he did need to smile more.

She got up and strolled close by his table and did a few twirls until she caught his attention. When she knew he was focused on her she changed her stance. She put her right hand by her forehead and left hand behind her and did an Egyptian walk. After strutting a few steps she flipped around with both her hands above her head. She squinted her eyes slightly while moving her head side to side. After finally getting a smile from her cute judge she Egyptian strutted back to the bench.

Alex had a big grin on his face, "you sure caught his attention, he keeps peeking over at you."

"Well, I am enjoying humoring him, and you too," she poked at her brother.

"You should talk to him."

Allie shrugged her shoulders, "maybe." She really wanted to but did not want to come across as overzealous. She was beyond ready to meet people, even if nothing came of it she had to jump in and start somewhere. She studied him a little more watching his reaction as each girl came up to the table. He seemed to be able to do a quick assessment before making a note. After that he seemed a little disinterested, looking around, leaning back and not making any comment to the other judges. She wondered if he always was judging the way people looked and what he possibly thought of her. She knew she made him smile and he seemed ready for another distraction. She got up and slowly stepped over into his sights again. She kept her shoulders slightly angled with her hands at her sides. She took each step with her toes pointed out in front of her. After a few steps she put her hands over her head and did a few ballerina spins. Only she was never a ballerina. On the last turn her heel slid out and she wobbled almost falling. She did not care though, she righted herself as she laughed and took a grand curtsy bow. She just hoped he did notice, she was not able to catch a good view of him as she spun around. She wanting to make him laugh again, not just look foolish for the rest of the crowd hanging around.

When she did finally catch his eye he was in fact laughing but in a nice way. He gave her a small round of applause before holding one finger up at her indicating for her to wait. She watched him scribble a note, when he held it up it read 'meet me in 15'. Allie gave him another curtsy and a smile and managed her best model walk back to the bench.

She grabbed her brothers hand and pulled him up, "come on, I need to freshen up, he wants to meet me in fifteen minutes."

James watched the woman leave after shuffling his papers back in order. Honestly he could not remember how they even ended up on the floor. He wondered if he would have noticed her if they had not swooshed off his desk. Probably he decided, she was eye catching. And he was used to having women try to grab his attention both personally and professionally. He was not quite sure which one she was trying to accomplish. She did not carry herself like a model and she was just a touch too big for the runway. Which did not mean he did not appreciate her figure. She was tall and fit with the right amount of curves any woman should have. So that left with her vying for his personal attention, maybe. All types of women did all sorts of weird things In the hopes of landing a modeling contract. Most of the time he ignored them. He wondered why he considered talking to her again. He glanced at her one more time noting her soft layered blonde hair with long bangs. He was pretty sure the eyes that sparkled at him were blue and her clear skin glowed with almost no make up. Of course he knew many of these types of women. So why was she different?

He tried to focus his attention back on the contest. He kept looking to see if she was there, see if she would come back to entertain him some more. That was it. She made him smile, something he had not been doing much of lately. Sure he lived a good life, surrounded by beautiful women but lately he seemed to be just going though the motions. But that was by choice, a choice he wanted to stick with. When she showed back up he would give his usual you are not what the agency is looking for speech and send her on her way.

The contest ended and James packed up his paperwork, keeping some head shots of models he might contact in the future. He stepped off the stage to see the woman coming towards him. She was smiling and full of energy he thought as he watched her toss her long shimmering hair behind her shoulders. Then his cynical self came back in figuring she would be handing him her personal info in hopes of a job. Still he was the one who asked her to come back so he would at least find out what she wanted from him.

"Hi, all done judging?" He was greeted enthusiastically.

"Um, yeah, you know you could have just signed up for the contest." He wanted to know quickly what her angle was.

Allie looked at him a little quizzically, "who me? Oh no, I am too old," she responded making up any excuse. She knew she was attractive but certainly not in the realm of fashion model.

James knew she was right, not that she looked old by any means though he knew better than to pretend to guess a woman's age. "We take women of all ages," he told her throwing in a half a smile to make it sound more convincing.

"Well then, I am sure I am too short, too fat or too something. In any case I have a job."

"So you are not trying to land a modeling contract?" he asked her quizzically.

"No, I told you I have a job. I am a manager at the new Blue Towers Hotel. I take it you are some sort of modeling agent then?"

"Scout, mentor, agent. Sorry, I am just used to women trying all sorts of things to get my attention."

"Not just professionally I am sure," she added a little laugh to keep the conversation light.

James responded with just a small smile while looking away. He still was not sure where the conversation was going. He needed to get back to his office yet he could not seem to find a way to walk away.

Allie waited for a moment more for a response. When she did not get one she figured it was time to make a move. "I have to work in a few hours but I have time for coffee if you want to join me and my brother."

"I need to get back to the office." Saying that a little too matter of fact he immediately regretted it, he just did not know what else to say.

She was still hopeful, "well my name is Allie and I am new in town. I am just trying to meet people, maybe find someone who can show me around some." She thought if she put it on a friend level he might be more receptive.

"Nice to meet you, I am James," he said offering his hand. He did not however offer any additional response to her. Even if she was not flirting with him he was not sure he wanted to pursue a friendship either.

Allie decided to give it one more chance and then she would let it go. Good looks aside she really did want to make friends also. "Well James, another day for coffee? Or shall we chance another random meeting in this big city of millions of people?"

He stepped back crossing his arms over his chest. He hardened his eyes while thinking about his response. After a moment he said, "I think I will chance another random meeting."

Allie kept her smile, "it was nice meeting you, I am glad I made you smile." She turned and bit her lip. She managed to keep her head high as she walked back to her brother. After all it was just her first attempt at meeting someone and ultimately it was probably not the right circumstance. Still, you never know where you might meet the right person Allie reminded herself. She remembered when her brother met Katie while she was on vacation and they just met up through her roommate. She smiled at the thought of Emma and her boyfriend Ben and the tough time they went through and are now working through the long distance. She was genuinely happy for Emma and her brother, it just made her more ready to get out and find someone for herself.

She checked the time and realized it was time to send her brother to meet his girlfriend and for her to get to work. Allie wrapped her arm through her brother's and pulled him up. "Come on lover boy time to go see Katie."

Without hesitation Alex jumped up, he was excited though he was here for his sister as well. "So do you have a date?"

"No," Allie said winding their way though the crowds to get back to the escalators.

"Really? What did he say?"

"Nothing really, I guess he is not interested. It's fine. Plenty more men to meet," she made a grand arm gesture at all the people walking by.

Alex smiled at his sister giving her a boost of confidence, "he's here, you will find him."

"Thanks," Allie added a little extra spring to her step, James sure was sexy though. His image would be hard to let go from her memory.

"Maybe Katie knows some cute doctor she could hook you up with."

Allie smiled at that, "come on I will make sure you get on the right train before I head to work."

James did not want to stop back at the office, he wanted to go home put his feet up and have a cold beer. He ignored all requests to go out and party. He was tempted to shut his phone down completely but that generally was not an option. He could at least screen everything coming in and if anything was truly important he would wait for a message.

Judging modeling contests was not his idea of fun, he only agreed as a last minute favor. He had been bored most of the afternoon. He did not agree with who the winner should be but he was only one of four judges that day. Sure she was the classically beautiful All-American teen, in his opinion she would only last for a short time. Modeling was like fashion, trends changed quickly and he was good at predicting trends. For him it did not really matter who won. He had a few photos in his bag of the young women who he thought had more potential.

He stopped by his secretaries' desk. Cheryl was his lifeline, she fielded all of his calls, sent out the rejections and overall made his life easier. She was a family friend and when she fell on hard times his parents recommended her for the job. She definitely proved herself worthy. The only downside was that she could be a busy body with his personal life. James was all right with it as long as she kept everything running smoothly for him.

He handed over the bios for Cheryl to start working on. She would check their work histories and their social media sites. He was always willing to work with new models but they had to be professional, he did not put up with any nonsense being posted on the Internet.

"Hey sweetie," she was the only one allowed to call him that, "how did it go?"

James shrugged his shoulders, "usual types. Can you start looking into these for me?" He pointed to the envelope he handed over.

Cheryl took a quick glance at her watch, "do you mind if it waits until Monday? I have a date tonight."

He smiled at her. He guessed her to be in her early fifties, she kept her spiky hair dyed red and was well dressed. After her ex husband cheated on her she started running and lost weight. Then she re-imagined herself. He wondered if Allie would look as good in twenty five to thirty years. He guessed she would. He pictured her long blond hair and sparkle in her eyes when she laughed. She made his afternoon tolerable. So why did he turn her down for coffee? She said she was just looking for a friend, a tour guide in a way. Well he had enough going on his life, he did not need another person or thing that needed attending. On the other hand she did make him smile and not one person or thing had done that to him for quite some time.

"Hello, earth to James," Cheryl finally managed to get his attention back.

"Oh sorry."

Cheryl let a small smile creep across her face, "I know that far off look, who is she?"

James squinted his eyes at her in annoyance for her being right. "No one." He grabbed a sticky note off her desk, she had them stuck everywhere. She was a little old fashion in that way. He did not care as long as she was efficient. He wrote a name and location on the small piece of square yellow paper and handed it over.

"Last thing before you go; I need you to get this message to this person," he pointed to the name on the paper.

"No one huh?" she raised her eyebrows at the man she loved like a son. "So does this no one get flowers to go with the message?"

"No, just find out her schedule, make the meeting two hours before and text me the time," he said sternly as he walked into his office.

Chapter 2

Allie walked into her office, it was small but it was hers and she felt she earned it. While she liked the beach, the last hotel she worked for was right on the ocean, New York City was a top tourist and business destination and she was determined to give its guests the best visit possible. Of course she was still learning her way around as well. She relied heavily on her staff to give the best advice to her clients. She also spent a lot of time doing her own research as well. Although that was mostly on the computer so she really was looking for more local input. She had a great visit with her brother and meeting James was a fun bonus even if she would not likely see him again. She allowed herself one more moment to remember how his features softened when he smiled. Now it was time to get back to work. Holiday season was approaching and parties were quickly booking up. She put James out of her mind and dug into her work.

A couple times per night Allie liked to get out of her office and stretch her legs. She personally greeted guests and made sure their needs were being met. She met with her staff as well and made sure they were happy and she always welcomed feedback. Since she was hired after most of the staff she wanted to get to know them on a more personal level.

The front desk clerks were especially important as they were the first point of contact for the visitors. Jenny was young and enthusiastic. Allie loved that she always smiled and connected with the clients. The downside was trying to keep her from chit chatting too much. But if that was her biggest fault Allie would deal with it.

She made a stop back by the front desk to observe the staff and greet the guests. When Jenny had a free moment she walked over to Allie. "You have a secret admirer," Jenny told her.

Allie looked at her quizzically, "why would you say that?"

Allie watched Jenny walk back to the desk and pull something out from the shelf. After a few moments of keeping her focus on the object she realized it was a single pink rose with a note attached to it. She looked at the card to make sure it was actually addressed to her. Again, she did not know too many people yet.

"What does it say?" Jenny asked practically jumping up and down in excitement.

Allie smirked back then she opened the card and read it out loud. "There could be a chance for a random encounter at 66th and Columbus around 12 pm tomorrow afternoon." She was in shock, it could have only come from James. She smelled the rose. She was a little confused about what it meant but she would not over think it.

"Who is it from?"

Allie quickly put the card back in the envelope, "someone I met earlier today. Honestly I did not think anything would come of it. And it still may not."

"And what about the rose that came with it?"

"I don't know, it does not seem to fit."

"Are you going to go?"

"Oh yes, I will be there." Allie turned and smiled to herself adding a bit of extra bounce as she headed back to her office.

The next morning Allie did her best to adhere to her usual routine while taking a few minutes to catch up with her brother and her last roommate Emma. They were both happy for her, they also wanted her to be cautious. Allie understood, however they were meeting in the middle of the day when there would be plenty of people around. The meeting place was not too far from where she had been with her brother. Other than that she was not sure what else was there. She did not know if they were meeting for lunch or if it was to show her something tourist related. The time was right but the card did not mention anything about food. Maybe it was work related for him. Either way she also had to be ready for work. She would not have enough time to come all the way back.

She rummaged through the tiny closet. She did not like the way her clothes were packed in so tight. It was on her shopping list to resolve the situation. Even just a simple wardrobe rack would do. Allie did not feel like she spent her money frivolously but she did spend extra money on her clothes so she would always look professional and current. Not that she was complaining, she knew how lucky she was that she did not have to search for an apartment. Her friend Molly graciously was letting her stay there for a year while she settled in to her new life. Eventually she would have to muddle through the real estate world. Competition was fierce for good apartments. For now though creating a social life was a high priority.

She decided on a quick snack before heading out to catch the downtown train. If there was no food involved she would grab something to go to bring to her office. She stepped outside to a cool breeze and a warm sun making for a lovely afternoon. The rain from the previous day gave the city a freshness that could lift anyone's mood. Too bad it did not translate to her subway station. She figured since not too many tourists came up this far north it was low priority in keeping it clean. She pursed her lips as she watched a rat the size of a cat scurry across the tracks. As long as they kept to themselves she would get over it she thought to herself as she put on her headphones and waited for the train.

The meeting spot was only a few blocks from Columbus Circle where Allie got off the train. Having taken the express train she was running a little ahead of schedule. She took her time and noted what was in the area. She had invested in an iPad mini that she carried everywhere with her. She was starting a list of trendy shops, restaurants and entertainment. Allie reached the corner just before twelve. Looking around she noted they were just a block off Lincoln Center and the equally famous Juliard school. There was also a hot dog cart that was making her stomach rumble, otherwise she was not sure what else she was there for. And since there were four corners to every intersection she decided to not cross and stood on the first corner and kept her eye out for James.

James was hoping to make the meeting quick. Not that he had another place to be in particular, he just was not sure what made him set this up. He knew enough people, had enough in his life to keep himself busy. He did not feel like he had room for another person texting, calling, trying to make plans, trying to solve his problems. After a quick greeting he would let her know she would have to seek a local guide elsewhere.

Of course that is what he planned on saying until he saw her. He slowed his walk down just a touch so he could glance at her a little longer. The slim black skirt and blue sweater wrap showed off her curves. Curves that made her a woman and not the girlish figures he was used to being around all day. He was surrounded by the most extraordinary females all day long. Allie could be just another face in the crowd to him.

So why did he keep going towards her he thought to himself. He could easily turn around, walk away, go on with his life. And as she indicated it was unlikely they would run into each other again. He hesitated trying to make a quick decision but then she turned boasting a beautiful smile that sent a jolt through him. It was like her bright eyes and big smile were sending rays of happiness. Which he did not want, he liked living in his dark world. He ran his hand through his long hair shaking off the nerves he was not accustomed to feeling.

Allie was feeling a little nervous herself. She was not entirely sure how to greet him. Definitely not a hug, a handshake seemed too business like and for all she knew he was one of those people that did not like physical contact. She laughed at that causing her to smile. Well, she hoped not. That would be a problem especially since she just caught sight of him coming up the street. He had that New York walk: confident and purposeful. Yet there was a hesitation. He was watching her without focusing as if he did not want to be caught. Allie decided to have a little fun to avoid the possibility of tension.

She started heading his way and when she was within a few feet of him she smiled tilting her head. "James? Is that you? Fancy meeting you here." She stopped just in front of him keeping her hands on the straps of her messenger bag.

James looked back her, relieved and humored. "Do I know you?" he asked playing along. "Wait it's coming back to me, walk like an Egyptian girl?"

"That would be me," she replied doing a quick Egyptian hand pose. "It's funny, I was just hanging around on the corner, just, um," she looked around trying to come up with something, "hanging out and here you are."

He eyed her with a touch of suspicion, "either you are soliciting men or you got my note."

"Or you found out this is my corner this weekend." After she said that she noticed James looking a little uneasy. She started laughing, "I'm just kidding, obviously you know I work at the hotel. Thanks for the rose by the way."

James dropped his head putting his hands on his hips, he loved Cheryl and he should have known that she would take this too far. "It was supposed to be just the note."

Allie suspected that so she was not disappointed, "I thought so. Obviously someone cares about you. It was a nice gesture."

James did not respond and was looking a little too serious again. Allie looked around again wanting to change the course of the conversation. "So what is so special about this corner?"

He pointed to the opposite side of the intersection, "the hot dog cart. It's one of my favorites. Are you hungry?"

"Yes, let's go." Allie had not yet tried one of the famous New York dogs.

As they walked closer the aroma was making her stomach growl. Every time the vendor lifted the lid she could see the steam rising which sent a new wave of aroma through the air. It was not gourmet cooking but she had been wanting to try one for a while. She leaned closer to James and asked softly, "don't they call these dirty water dogs?"

"Sshh," he gestured with his finger, "they don't like to hear that. Besides I think the health department started making them change the water every day," he added with a smile. "Do you want anything on it?"

"Sauerkraut, and a coke too please."

"Diet?"

"No, good old fashion Classic Coke."

"I like that, all the girls drink diet after eating the donut." He ordered their food and paid. "Lets cross over by Lincoln Center, we can sit on the steps if that is all right with you."

They crossed over and came to a plaza with three buildings in a u shape. In the center was a round pool with a fountain. Finding a spot warmed by the sun they sat and started digging into their lunch before the dogs cooled off. Allie leaned over as she bit into it in case the sauerkraut started to drip. She wiped the corners of her mouth while she watched James devour his in about four bites.

When he was finished he asked, "how is it?"

She nodded as she was still chewing. "It's good," the hot dog was juicy without being soggy or rubbery, the sauerkraut added the right extra flavor and the bun stayed dry. She hated soggy bread. "I can see why they are so popular."

After she finished off the last of the hot dog she looked over at the performing arts center. She knew ballets, operas and concerts took place there. "Maybe I will go see The Nutcracker this year."

James looked over with her, "you should go, it is the best in the world," he stated as if everyone would know that.

"Have you seen it?"

He shrugged, "of course. My mom took me as a kid, she always said it is good to know about the things girls like. I think it was more because she wished I was a girl.

"Boys can be ballerinas."

"Uh huh, not this one. Not that I have anything against it, you just won't catch me in a pair of tights."

Allie looked down at his jeans covered legs thinking he could pull it off. His long lean body could easily glide across the stage and his strong but not bulky arms could lift a girl without a problem during a pas de deux "So what other girl things to do you know about?"

"I am a pretty good make up artist, I can do a mean French braid, I can accessorize any outfit," he suddenly stopped realizing he was responding without thinking about the fact he was sharing things about himself he did not normally. He noticed that Allie was eying him with a curiosity that he immediately answered, "no I am not gay. It just comes from having grown up in the fashion industry."

Allie laughed, "it's fine, just good to know. I get it, you're still a tough guy. So what manly things do you like then city boy?"

James was caught off guard, he had to think about that for a moment. He did not watch sports much, he did not own a car, he did not do outdoor adventure sports. When he did finally respond, he did so very seriously, "I like a good dark beer."

While James was thinking Allie realized she needed to head to work. She stood up and said, "James, you have redeemed yourself." She wished she did not have to leave and was hopeful for another meeting. "I had nice time, maybe we will meet again?"

James was not quite ready to leave either. He had scheduled the time to be fairly short on purpose. He was feeling relaxed, he enjoyed the light conversation that did not involve work or serious life provoking topics. Allie was in fact a nice distraction. "I think we may bump into each other again."

The Blue Towers Hotel Midtown was not too far from where Allie had just met James. It was still a little quicker to hop on the subway to get there versus walking. After getting back to street level and walking two more blocks she entered the high ceiling lobby feeling really good about the day and life in general. Even on days she was not having a good day the lobby of the hotel was inviting and comforting which of course was the way it should be. The floor was mostly dark wood with beechwood inlays. The furniture was bamboo and wood with plush cushions. There were places to meet up with friends and other areas to curl up with a book in private. She looked around briefly thinking it was almost time for a few fall decorations and some pumpkins.

As Allie walked by the reception desk she noticed Jenny looked a little distressed. She walked behind the desk and dropped her bag on the floor. There was a couple that appeared to be of retirement age standing on the other side. "Hi my name is Allie Golding, how is your stay?" She did recall seeing the couple in the lobby the day before so she knew they were not just checking in.

"We are missing cash from our room and before you start asking questions, no I did not lose it outside. I did not want to carry too much cash with me and I know I should have used the safe but I figured I should not have to worry about theft in the rooms."

"Sir you are absolutely right." Although Allie knew policy was for the hotel not to be responsible, she would need to investigate the staff. "Sir can you pinpoint the day the money went missing?"

"We checked in Thursday so it was between then and today."

Allie took a quick scan of the computer monitor and noted they were checking out on Tuesday. She would not be able to complete an investigation by then. She changed screens on the computer and hit the print button. She handed the form to the couple and had them fill out the formal complaint. They would eventually get a check from the corporate office but she needed to please the couple now.

"I told you not to leave the cash in the drawer," the wife said swatting at her husband.

Allie stifled a giggle, "I am sorry for any inconvenience, I will make sure to switch up the staff that enters your room and you will find a discount on your final bill. Is there anything else I can do for you right now?"

"No ma'am thank you. I know you don't have to believe us or do anything for that matter," the husband replied. He sighed heavily knowing the berating from his wife had only just begun.

And Allie knew thieves came in all shapes and sizes, colors and ages. Whether or not she believed was not the point, the hotel had just opened and she needed to maintain the reputation of the brand. "Well sir, we hold our staff to the highest integrity and if there is a problem it will be taken care of. Please let us know if we can do anything else for you."

After the couple left Allie turned to Jenny, "stop by my office when you get a chance."

She turned after she got the nod, Allie was glad there had been no one else at the desk to overhear. That's all she needed was for word to get out and for the new hotel to receive bad reviews.

Her day did not improve when she sat down at her desk. Holiday season was coming up and their banquet rooms were pretty well booked up. Since the hotel was new Allie wanted to prove they could host high end parties. If she could accomplish that it would translate into spring bridal season. As soon as she turned on her computer she saw there was an urgent message that one of their rooms was double booked on several days. Frustration kicked in, she walked into an unexpected train wreck with little time to fix it. Still, these were her first challenges and she was there to prove herself. She picked up the phone and started making calls.

After hours of negotiations and rescheduling Allie was able to fix the double bookings although she would still have to deal with how it happened in the first place. Which left the situation of having an employee stealing. She closed her eyes for a moment. It was getting late and she was tired. Her thoughts were drifting to James. She pictured his dark skin and dark piercing eyes. They were always searching, probably for the next great model but there was a sorrow in them as well. Just as she was wondering what the sadness could be she was wakened by a soft knocking on her door.

Allie was happy to see Jenny walk in. She asked her to help look into the theft situation. Jenny was always cheerful and made friends with everyone. That would help Allie out by giving her a feel of who might be the problem. If there was a problem. In a way she hoped not but she needed to know for sure. Certainly there would always be untruthful people out there who would try to get free rooms or other perks. It was close to the end of both of their shifts so she wanted to get right to the point. "What do you have for me?"

Jenny moved forward, shifting her hands from behind her back as she sat down. She presented her with a printout of which housekeepers and possible handymen may have entered the room the last three days. Oddly there seemed to be a hole with no record on the second day. They were set up to know who did each room but it seemed no one cleaned that room. She turned to her computer and pulled up the whole floor and there seemed to be random holes of rooms not being cleaned. Either there was a glitch in the computer system or with the staff.

"Did you get to talk to anyone today?"

"Sarah was out sick the last two days so not likely her. Andrea tends to keep tabs on everyone which could mean it was Harry from maintenance or maybe Rosa the housekeeper."

"All right, well I don't want to start accusing anyone and I don't want word to get out before I decide what to do." Even though Jenny could talk a lot Allie did trust her. "Thanks for the help." When Jenny did not get up Allie asked, "anything else?"

A smile crept slowly across Jenny's face. She reached behind her back and pulled out a small box with a note attached.

Allie reached across and opened the notecard. It was in a different handwriting than the previous note. She read it out loud figuring Jenny would be asking her anyway. "Thought you might like dessert, meet me at 45th and 6th Tuesday at 12 pm for more delicious bites. She immediately opened the box of Russell Stovers and picked the dark chocolate. She closed her eyes as she bit into strawberry cream and chocolate. "Chocolate makes everything better," she was not surprised James would know that being surrounded by women. She had no idea what the meaning was, she would just take it as a nice gesture for now. While they were not Godiva chocolates they certainly were not dollar store either. She handed the box over to Jenny and let her have a pick.

After Jenny licked the caramel off her fingers she smiled, "you have another date."

Allie closed the box and put it in her bag which she then slung over her shoulder. She stood up and responded, "I don't think I would call it a date but I can't wait to see what we are eating next."

Walking out of the hotel Allie was always grateful it was close to the subway stop and equally grateful her apartment was close as well. Leaving in the dark was the only downside to her shift. At least in midtown there were always people out and about especially on the weekends. It was much quieter where she lived and when she got off the train she always pulled out her keychain that had a small can of mace on it. While it was a quiet residential neighborhood you never knew what could happen. She walked briskly to her building and went inside. She stopped to pick up her mail and glanced through it. She was intrigued when she saw she received her second invitation for the day.

Chapter 3

Summer made a brief return forcing Allie to dig deeper into her small jam packed closet. She pulled out a long maxi dress and found a pair of matching sandals. She lathered on sunscreen and a light application of make up, grabbed her purse and was out the door. She was heading to Times Square and was looking forward to the people watching.

James had passed though Times Square thousands of times in his life. He was unimpressed with the tourists, unimpressed with the lights and billboards although it was a lot more cleaned up then it used to be. Sure there were still cheesy tourist shops and greasy hair guys passing out flyers for strip clubs. And the characters were on every street corner; Minnie, Mickey and Elmo were everywhere. He thought it would seem confusing for the kids for there to be multiples of the same character.

Even so he could see the lure for the visitors and that is why he chose this spot. With the influx of new stores and the closing off of some of the streets to car traffic the whole atmosphere changed. There were chairs and tables and stadium seating for people watching. James headed over to his food stand of choice and ordered lunch. He was not worried about ordering for Allie, he knew what the best dish was at the food truck.

He tucked two bottles of water under his arm and carried the trays over to the tables. He scanned for his lunch date and almost dropped the food when he saw Allie strolling towards his general direction. He was glad she did not see him. She was already a ray of sunshine on any day but with the sun shining on her golden hair he swore she was literally glowing. And there was always that look of happiness, perhaps a slight weariness this time but also a sense of well being. Much more than he could say for himself.

He put the lunch down before he fumbled again. He saw Allie look around so he took in an extra second to admire her feminine figure in her flowing dress. James shook his head, that was not why he was there. He needed to clear the air and quickly. When she turned his way he waved her over.

Allie was headed over to the designated spot but was equally looking around. Most tourists made a trip through Times Square so she wanted to get a better feel for the area. While she had passed through herself she spent a little more time to see what was actually there. It was daytime so the bright lights did not quite have the same effect. Still, the Broadway show signs and video screens gave the area a sense of motion and excitement. She looked up to see where the New Years Eve ball drops and smiled at the giant Coca Cola sign. As she looked around scanning the stores she caught James waving her over.

He already found a table and bought the food. She did not mind as she was always up for trying new things. What she still did not know was how to greet James. His expression was hard to read. He was watching her but almost seeing through her. She knew that it was only their second meeting, was she supposed to shake his hand? Too formal. Light hug? Too friendly. Ultimately she smiled and pulled out her own chair and sat down.

Allie was not sure what she was sensing from James, a slight discomfort was the only way she could describe it. She decided to focus on the food. "This smells great, are you sure you did not get take out from a restaurant?"

He managed a slight smile and let some of the tension he was feeling run out of his body. "Food truck on the corner," he said pointing behind him. "The best chicken, lamb and rice you will find anywhere."

Allie took in a forkful and closed her eyes as she took in the different flavors. The dish was moist and flavorful without being too spicy. "This is delicious."

They ate in silence for a few minutes. James mostly ate because the food was there. He finished his last bite and waited for Allie to finish as well. He jumped in and and started what he needed to say before he lost his nerve again. "I, uh, need to make something clear."

Allie took another drink of her water and looked at him. She knew something was up. Maybe he had a girlfriend and was telling her now, or he was not interested and was dumping her before they even had a real date. As long as he was honest she would take whatever he had to say. She clasped her hands on the table and waited to hear him out.

Damn if her eyes weren't still sparkling. It would have been easier if she looked mad, untrusting or uneasy, instead she sat with concern, curiosity and understanding. "Dating, I don't date." When he saw her look at him with one eyebrow raised he realized he was stumbling. "I mean, yes I like women, I am on dating break right now." James drank more of his water trying to drown out his nerves, which was ridiculous, women did not make him nervous.

That was news Allie could deal with. A little disappointing, she knew there was an attraction there. She would not push him though and she would not ask why right now. She was sure he had a good reason or at least he thought he did. At this point she would be more interested in learning about other parts of his life. If all he needed was a friend then she would be there. She could still use him to benefit her own needs. "That's fine, no problem. I would like to keep hanging out though, I enjoy your company."

He was not sure if he was relieved, upset, sad or mad. It would be easier to let her go, walk away. Somehow he could not, deep down he knew she was there to shake up his life. A shaking he was not sure he was ready for. Still the woman sitting across from him was a breath of fresh air for him. He might be playing a fine line trying to maintain just a friendship with her. He made the decision to not date a long time ago and would stand by it, he was still not ready. On the other hand, having a friend on the outside of his work world; that he was ready for. "I would like that."

"Good," Allie said perking up, "I just got an invite to an open house cocktail party tomorrow night. My roommate from Virginia, Emma, looks like her boyfriend is selling his place. According to my brother he is moving down there, it's only been a few months but they are in love," she stretched out the word love. "She does not know, and I can't tell which is killing me. I do think it will be better, her not knowing. If he asks her she will think too much about it."

James was amused, clearly she had a great friend. "Sounds like it is a good thing though. Just act surprised when she tells you."

"I will. Anyway will you go with me?"

"Sure, I always know someone looking for real estate."

"Great, I will send you the address and time, we can meet there." Allie looked at her watch figuring it would be time for him to get back to the office. "Do you have a lot of work to do today? Do you need to head back?" It was her day off and and she could use more time with her guide.

"Nope, actually I am technically working right now."

"Oh, well isn't that nice," she liked her job but it required her to be inside all the time. She looked around and understood, "well this would definitely be the place to people watch."

"Sometimes, too many tourists on most days. Truth is my bosses were not happy I did not pick up anyone from the model search. Quite honestly if I was truly interested I would have been on them that day. I sent a few inquiries but let them go out late."

"You are successful at your job though right, so should they not trust your judgement?"

"They do," he sighed. "There may have been one or two that would have had moderate success. I look for greatness, not average. My clients are very successful."

"Right and so......," she knew there must be more.

"And so maybe I have slacked off lately. Of course I still make the company plenty of money. You just never know when you lose someone to another agency or when they just might leave."

"Which means you have to keep searching. Always on the hunt for the new hottest face of the fashion world."

"Yup, something like that."

James stiffened slightly when Allie suddenly moved her chair very close to his. He generally liked his personal space but when he caught the scent of vanilla he closed his eyes and let himself take her in. When he opened them again her head was right next to his even though she was looking out into the small crowd of people. She said real quietly, "so tell me about the people walking by, how would you assess them?"

He looked out to the people walking by ignoring the obvious ones that would not fit in, "lets see, her shoulders are too stocky, her nose won't photograph well, her knees are too knobby. Eyes too close together, ears stick out, that guy is pretty good looking but I don't do guys. Too much testosterone in one room, does not work for me. Shall I keep going?"

Laughing slightly she said, "no. Does that ever turn off? Or do you do that all the time?" She had a mild curiosity as to what he would say about her, not that she would dare to ask.

"I guess it's more of a subconscious thing. It's not like I go around saying everyone's faults. It's more that I know what I am looking for, so when I see that person then I kick into work mode. Come on, lets take a walk."

"Can we go in the M&M's store, please?" she asked clapping her hands like a little kid. She knew it was silly but she loved the chocolate candy.

Once inside the store she was salivating over the wall of every possible color of mini chocolates. Far more choices that came in the store bags. There were also color combinations from pink breast cancer awareness to the yellow, grey and black taxi combo. She grabbed a bag and started filling.

James grabbed her arm before she got her first candy. "You are not actually going to buy these?"

"Yes I am," she responded with defiance.

"You know it's cheaper at the corner drug store."

Allie shrugged her shoulders, "I know but where can you get these colors?" She filled her bag to the top.

"Well if you want to play tourist when you are done with that we will go and do a real tourist thing."

Popping her colorful candies into her mouth Allie followed James across the street over to the giant Toys R' Us store. She almost dropped her candy when they spun through the entrance door and walked into the main floor which was partly a balcony. Allie walked over to the railing and looked down then up at the three story tall ferris wheel that went down a street level and up above their heads. She smiled at the different cars; from the M&M's car to My Little Pony. She also delighted in the Barbie convertible, fire truck and the red and yellow buggy car.

She turned to James with the biggest grin, "we have to ride that."

"Wait here, I will get us tickets."

When he came back James took Allie to see more of the big toys. She was looking all around as they rode the escalator up. A loud rumble suddenly overtook the whole area causing Allie to jump back. Luckily for her James was a step behind her. He caught her and helped her regain her balance as they stepped off onto solid ground. She turned around still in his arms.

Laughing she said, "I knew it was there, I saw it in pictures but it still caught me off guard." Allie was referring to the life size T. Rex that was warning everyone off. She was not sure how younger kids made it up the escalator without breaking down in tears.

"Gets you every time." James smiled back at the youthful joy in her eyes. He would have stood there much longer looking at her, watching her joy, her silliness, except for the flow of people coming up behind them. He guided her off to the the side then let go. He probably could have kept hold of her arm in an amicable way. Plenty of friends link arms with no issues, or so he noticed. That was not his style though. Men and women should have boundaries. Friendship has boundaries and he planned on making that very clear.

Not that she noticed his actions, her head was on swivel. Of course she was beyond buying toys but who could resist the T. Rex, and the Superman and the Statue of Liberty made of Legos? They wandered through the aisles commenting on toys old and new and how some evolved and some have remained the same. Making their way into the girls section and seeing all the pink ahead Allie was immediately brought back to her childhood. Allie had her Barbie dolls and Alex had his action figures. She laughed thinking about Barbie battling monsters and aliens, shooting semi automatic weapons and parachuting from the top of the bookcases. It was the only way her brother would let her play with him. Of course when he would leave the room, Barbie and her comrades were a little more intimate. In her world, Barbie had not met Ken yet so it was never an issue. Her Barbie would take GI Joe for rides in her convertible. Their dates would have to end abruptly as Alex would not tolerate girl mush. And now he was the one in love.

Allie came back to the present and continued her journey through the Barbie wonderland. She literally entered the dream house she never got to have as a kid. She ran up the spiral staircase that led to the second floor balcony. As she looked down she could not tell what James was doing or looking at. She yelled down to him, "oh Romeo, Romeo where are thou my Romeo?"

James did a quick look around and yelled back, "nope I don't see him here. And please do not let down your hair either." He noticed the slight glare she tossed back at him so he added with a smile, "you know it might actually hurt if I used your hair as a rope."

"You're no fun," Allie said as she flipped her hair over her shoulder and turned back. She came back down the stairs and started wandering through the aisles, noting all the different styles and new toys. If she ever has a daughter, she will get Barbie dolls, not all the new big head puffy lip kind. Allie smiled at her memories and possible future and headed out of the house. She noted a distracted James and headed his way.

"Wishing you were Ken?" Allie asked in a teasing manner.

It took a moment for James to register what she said. He played along this time, "lets see, she has a convertible, a camper, a boat, a nice house, can do any job, sure why not?" he smiled. But there was something, or someone more like it, that did catch his attention. He turned back to Allie, "do you want to help me?"

"Sure," maybe he needed to buy a gift for a relative Allie thought to herself.

"See that girl over there? Tall, slender with the red hair?" He waited for Allie to nod, "she is going to be my next model. Go over and talk to her."

Allie looked at him quizzically, "what do you want me to say? I thought that was your job."

"It is but sometimes you have to be careful how you approach young women, I don't want to be the weird stalker in the toy store. Just find our where she is from, if she is with her parents and then I can step in."

Allie wandered over to the girl not sure what to say. She did notice she was quite striking, not noticeable right away but with the right lighting she could see how she would photograph very well. Obviously James was good at his job. She could also see his point on being careful to not come across as a stalker. Especially since the girl appeared to be in her early to mid teens. Like herself, she seemed to be caught between being too old for the dolls but longing to hang on to the days of fantasy play.

Being careful not to stare too long, Allie noticed some of her favorite Barbie's where the girl was standing. She casually moved closer and picked up a box. "I love these vintage styles," she said directing her comment to the girl whose life was potentially about to change.

The girl nodded back politely. Allie picked up another box then remembered it was a weekday. "Are you here on vacation? I just moved here and it is my first time in this store. The T. rex freaked me out coming up the elevator."

That seemed to relax her a bit as she smiled, "my dad does business here, sometimes he brings us with him."

"Where are you from?"

"Rhode Island. We live in Providence, small city, not quite like here. I have been to this store a couple of times. I know what you mean about the dinosaur. Anyway, I don't play with my Barbies much anymore but I usually come to see what is new. I have most of the holiday versions."

Allie smiled as her new friend relaxed and talked about her doll collection. When she paused she jumped in and asked, "are your parents here now?"

"Oh yeah, they are in Lego land, my cousin loves Legos, they always buy him a new set when we come. I think it drives my Aunt Jackie crazy, so many small pieces everywhere but my mom does not care."

"Do you have any brothers or sisters?"

"No, I am an only child, my mom could not have anymore kids after me. Her sister has four kids so she likes to spoil them also."

Allie was not looking to get too personal and she needed to get to the point, "that is nice of her, my name is Allie by the way, what is yours?"

"Kelsey."

"Well it is nice to meet you, do you see that guy standing over there?" Allie nodded in James direction.

Kelsey looked over with wide eyes, "he's cute, is he your boyfriend?"

Allie smiled at her, "no, just a friend."

"Well he should be, is there something wrong with him?"

Allie broke out into a laugh, "not that I am aware of, we just met really. Anyway he is a model scout and he wants to talk to you."

Eyebrows raised and looking skeptical, "me? No way. I am the skinny, geeky kid at school."

"James is very good at his job, he knows beauty when he sees it." Allie looked over at James and nodded for him to come over.

Allie noticed Kelsey becoming shy and a bit nervous all of a sudden. "Don't worry, He is a good guy and he will want to talk to your parents as well. James this is Kelsey, Kelsey, this is my friend James."

The two shook hands just as Kelsey's parents called her name. James took out his business card and handed one to each of them. Allie watched and listened as James turned all business. He explained how he carefully monitored the younger girls and made sure they were treated well and that they themselves stayed out of trouble. He wanted to set up a photo shoot to see how she would do in front of the cameras. Kelsey's parents were obviously a little skeptical and ambivalent of the industry. But what parent could resist the eyes of their pleading daughter? They at least agreed to a second meeting with a photo shoot before they left town.

Kelsey turned to Allie and gave her a big hug, "thank you." Then she turned to James and politely shook his hand, "and thank you. And you should ask her out." She quickly turned away before anyone noticed her blushing and went off with her parents.

Allie looked at James, "you should ask me out."

"What? We are out. And now work can lay off me. And you got your M&Ms. And tomorrow is the open house right?"

"Yes, then I have to go back to work and catch a thief."

"Well now I have to get back to the office. Let me know if I can help."

Allie looked at him for a moment, her hopes not completely dashed that they would go on a real date someday, for now he was definitely a keeper as a friend. "I know, since you are such a great judge of people maybe you can help me find a date." Allie smiled at him and turned quick before he could answer, "see you tomorrow," she waved back at him, it was time for her ferris wheel ride.

That was not quite the type of help he was thinking of. He was stumped for words and James was glad he did not have time to answer. While he did not necessarily want to see Allie with another man it would take the pressure off him.

Chapter 4

Allie popped another yellow M&M into her mouth. She brought a dish from home and filled it with the rest of her pricey candies. The next bag would be from the supermarket, still there were some things you had to do at least once. Even though it was her day off she stopped by her office to check in on the situation with the theft problem. She learned there had been no additional reported problems which was a good thing. Maybe nothing would come of it, maybe the couple had made a mistake. She was not ready to make any accusations either way, nor did she want to make any of the staff suspicious. If there was a problem she wanted to take care of it quietly. For now the general manager agreed to let her resolve the issue since it happened on her watch.

She was going through the list of employees and their work histories when Jenny popped her head in. Allie motioned for her to come in and sit down. She offered her a candy which she readily took almost a handful of. Allie took the dish back before they all disappeared.

Jenny smiled at the motion, "been hanging out in Times Square?"

"Yes," Allie answered matter of fact keeping her focus on the profiles.

"Yeah, and how is mystery man?" Jenny asked reaching for another handful of candy.

Allie knew she would have to give up something if they were going to get on with the real business. "Mysterious for sure, something is holding him back. We just met though so I won't push him."

"Going to see him again?"

"Tonight," she decided to give her the bit of intrigue she was looking for, "and I told him he could help me find a date."

Jenny popped another candy into her mouth and contemplated for a moment. "You know that might backfire on you. He may just do that."

"Well then I guess I can't lose." And just as Allie wondered if that was true or not her phone rang. Another guest was reporting a theft.

By the time the reports were taken and Allie finished another round of researching the employees there was not enough time to go back home then come all the way back downtown. She looked reasonable enough wearing casual business attire. She did brush out her hair and add a little extra eye make up. You never knew where you would meet someone and a cocktail party was as good a place as any.

She took a short train ride then walked the few blocks to Ben's building. She remembered when she had to force Emma to go inside and make up with him. She did give herself some of the credit for getting them back together and now they were a happy couple. If she had said that out loud someone might have detected a slight jealousy to her tone, she knew that and was okay with it. Her time was coming she thought to herself as she opened the door. She was happy to see James waiting for her in the lobby. She pushed her thoughts aside and admired the man standing there. Allie took the moment as he was busy on his phone and he had not noticed her arrival. He wore a dark long overcoat which was sitting open revealing a charcoal fitted sweater and black slacks. He looked sleek and sophisticated which was making Allie's body quickly warm up from the cool night.

It was indeed James' job to notice people. And he did notice when Allie came in the door. And he also noticed when she stopped to look him over. He had in fact been sending a text on his phone but he pretended to keep typing so he could reciprocate the gesture. Looking sleek yet business like in the white wool coat and black slacks and heels, it was not quite what he expected but he liked the sophistication. The same sparkle in her eyes was still there, it was enhanced by a little extra makeup that was not overdone. Was it for him or was she serious about him helping her find a date?

When James put his phone back in his coat pocket Allie started towards him. She smiled when he noticed. She tried not to look over anxious even though with every step she took towards him she could feel her body heating up. She kept thinking she better find a date soon or else she would self implode. She did feel that she knew him well enough now to greet him with a hug. It also allowed her to take in his scent of musky aftershave. She felt her fingers tingle and her body shivered when he hugged her back. She wondered if it was just him or her lack of dating. She was ready to test the waters. "I am glad you came tonight."

James shrugged his shoulders, "no problem. Even though I am not looking right now I will keep my ears open for anyone that is. Besides I need to make sure no creepy guys start hitting on you."

They got in the elevator and Allie pressed the floor number, "I am sure Ben will appreciate that." She pauses giving James a questioning look, "how do I know you won't lie?"

Shrugging his shoulders he said, "I don't know, I guess you will have to trust me. Besides, the sooner you find a date, the sooner you can be rid of me."

"Oh no worries, you are stuck with me either way," Allie said with a smile as she hooked her arm into his and walked out into the hallway. Even if she was not going to be the one for him she still saw a special relationship developing. For now it was time to change the subject. "So how was your meeting with Kelsey and her parents?"

Grateful for something else to talk about he told her how well she photographed and with a little more guidance he thought she would do really well. He thought she would land a few jobs very quickly. Her parents would of course have the right to refuse any job first.

The pair reached Ben's door which was slightly ajar so they entered. They were greeted by a very cheerful real estate agent. She welcomed them with a glass of champagne. They entered the small foyer and passed their coats to an assistant who was hanging them in the closet. It was a nice touch to see that there was closet space, which is often a problem in city apartments. Allie wondered how much Ben had to pack away for the evening. Of course if he was leaving he had to pack up anyway. She noticed him putting out appetizers on the dining room table and headed his way.

He saw her coming and they embraced with big smiles. "It is so good to see you Ben. I can't believe you are leaving."

Bens eyes widened slightly, "you have not told Emma have you?"

"No, it's killing me though."

"Well it is killing me not being with her all the time. I know it has not been very long but I love her. I figure if I show up with a little Doberman puppy in hand, how could she say no?"

"She might keep the puppy and kick you to the curb," Allie said with a smile. When Ben's look turned sour she assured him, "you don't have anything to worry about. She loves you just as much. Well good luck selling this place, my friend James will let you know if he knows anyone who is looking."

After introducing the two she headed over to two of the other few people she knew. "Hi Molly, Jason, how is married life?"

Molly sassily smiled in return, "it is good."

"And teaching, kids treating you well?" Allie would always be grateful to Molly who was letting her use her old apartment for a year while she adjusted to city life.

"It has been tough, a bit more work then I expected. Also it is hard knowing that I can only do so much to help the kids but I know I can give them guidance and support while I have them." Molly made a point to take a job at a school with underprivileged kids, having a tough time herself growing up.

"You are a good woman and you are a lucky man Jason."

"He knows," Molly said with a smile. "How is the apartment?"

"Perfect," Allie answered graciously. A little small and out of the way but she would never complain about free rent for a year. "You know how much I appreciate you letting me use it."

"Someday you will find your own way to give back. On a different note, anything strange ever happen there?"

"No." Allie could not think of anything. There was a time when a coffee mug fell to the floor but she assumed that was her fault.

Molly hesitated then said, "my little sister can sometimes have some fun with people. And she can be opinionated, totally harmless though. I understand if you don't want to stay in the apartment."

Allie remembered that Molly's sister died many years ago. She never had a ghostly experience and did not necessarily want to. She did not want to give up free rent either. "As long as she is harmless."

The friends hugged then Allie made her way to the dining table and made herself a small plate of food. When she turned around she was greeted by a tall, very handsome man watching her. She took a short nervous breath as his dark eyes studied her.

"I know you from somewhere," he said further checking her out.

Allie could not place him, "I don't think so, I have not lived here for very long."

His look became more concentrated, "I don't forget faces and I surely would not have forgotten yours." After another moment of contemplation his eyes suddenly brightened. "Emerald green dress at Jason's wedding."

"Wow you are good." Allie studied the man then remembered, "we danced together, Lewis right?"

"That is right," he rewarded her with a brilliant smile. "And now you live here?"

"I moved here a few weeks ago."

"Well you make a lovely addition to this city," he said stepping in a little closer.

But before Allie could react in anyway Molly pushed herself in between the two. "This man is an ass and he is engaged."

"Oh come on Molly, I am just extending hospitality to our newest resident."

"Back off Lewis!" Molly, even though quite a bit shorter, managed to stare him down until he backed away. After which she sent one last grin and wink Allie's way.

"Sorry, I could not let him hit on you."

Allie was only slightly disappointed, "I would rather know now, so thanks. But if you know a good man send him my way." She picked up her plate and searched out James. She spotted him standing by himself at the living room window, arms crossed looking distant. Allie grabbed his elbow to catch his attention, she was not sure what he was focused on but it sure was not her this time. "Hey, what do you think of the apartment?"

"What?" Jason turned bringing his attention back, "oh sorry, it is pretty nice, good location. I think a two bedroom would be easier, the buyer could bring in roommates if needed. Still, for the price it should sell quickly. Who was that guy talking to you?"

Allie noticed his eyes harden. "Apparently no one worthy of my time. Or could you tell that?"

"As a matter of fact I could and if your friend did not intervene I was getting ready to knock him out."

"Do I detect a sense of jealousy?" She asked in a light manner.

"No, but I can detect a creep, I saw another woman hanging onto him when you were talking to Ben."

"Oh yes, you are forever observing people." Allie wondered if that was the fiancé he saw Lewis with. Not that it mattered, "see anyone worthy then?"

"Nope, which means it is my time to go. Lunch tomorrow?"

"Sure, I am going to stick around a bit though. See you tomorrow then."

James hesitated for a moment, "are you sure, it is getting late, you will be all right getting back by yourself?"

Allie smiled at his concern, "thanks I will be fine."

"Text me when you get back," James gave her one more look that he was serious before walking out the door.

A short time later, Allie was snuggled in her warm bed getting ready to turn off her light on her nightstand. As she reached over to hit the switch her phone fell to the floor. Odd, she did not recall hitting it. She picked it up grateful the face did not break on the ancient parquet floor. Could it be she wondered? A little ghost girl, a little girl reminding her to text James? She wondered if this little ghost girl was expressing her opinion about James as Molly said she might. She rubbed her eyes, why was she wondering what a little ghost thought anyway. What she thought was that it was nice of him to be there even though it was for a short time and it was nice of him to be concerned about her getting home even though she managed everyday after work. Would any guy be the same way? Maybe her brother but probably not most. She sighed, not wanting to overthink it or send anything cryptic she typed in, 'snuggled in tight good night.' Seconds later a smiley face was returned.

Allie was sitting in her office shuffling through e-mails and messages. Her lunch with Jame was uneventful. Good, a street cooked gyro dripping with white sauce, but uneventful. No further insight into his broodiness or lack of desire to date. And no comment on the previous evening. Oh well, if nothing else she was eating good food; fatty and fried but good.

Now what to do about the theft problem. She had a list of potential suspects and she did not want any other guests to get victimized. She needed a set up situation. Someone to stay as a guest.

"Don't you think it would be weird having him hanging around here?"

Jenny was referring to the idea of using James as the bait. To Allie, it seemed the perfect solution. He did offer to help and she certainly would not have him leave anything of true value in the room; the hotel would provide that. "He would just be another guest and we would have to pretend not to know each other. Holiday season is coming up and we need to get this done. And you need to keep your ears open," she gave Jenny a more serious look, "but stay quiet also."

"Hey, I don't even know what James looks like. But," she added more slowly, "I bet I will be able to pick him out. Maybe I can get him to talk," she added with a smile.

Allie tapped her fingers on her desk. On one hand she would not mind a little insight, on the other, it could back fire. "No need, and no flirting. Now go back to work."

"Do I get room service?" James asked the next day between popping roasted chestnuts in his mouth. They were wandering around midtown, lunch break for him and on the way to work for her. There were many vendors that sold roasted nuts. They all pretty much tasted the same.

"How about a small spending account? I would not want to spoil you by letting you get the most expensive menu items and a whole bottle of wine."

"I drink beer remember?"

"Yes I know, only the good stuff. So are you in?"

"And no contact inside the hotel?"

"Or right outside."

"Sounds fun to me. In the mean time I have an invite to a gallery opening next week, want to go?"

"Yes I would love to." If she could she would jump up and down and clap her hands, that was exactly the kind of event she wanted to attend. Instead she nodded and added, "that works out since the set up will not happen until late next week anyway."

James stood outside the art gallery waiting for Allie. They had not seen each other since sharing chestnuts the previous week. He wanted to back off for a few days, his mind was becoming clouded; especially by the fact that she did not push him at all. He knew she was interested in being more than friends but that was all he was capable of at the moment. He would have to figure out what was the right amount of contact that would sustain a friendship. She never seemed upset if they went a few days without talking. He also knew he would likely be replaced sooner or later. He hoped not, he wanted to keep her as a friend even knowing that it could get complicated if she did find a boyfriend. And if things did not work out James reminded himself he was fine before he met her and would be fine again if that is what it came down to.

He looked at the advertisement for the show while he was waiting, Torrid was the name. He had no interest in the art itself, he just happened to know the artist and the gallery owner. He silently laughed, he knew Allie was holding in her excitement. This was what she was looking for: a night out, a true city happening.

He ran his hand through his hair thinking it was another strange weather day with humidity hanging in the air and temperatures refusing to fall with the setting sun. Fall was precarious that way. No graceful drops in temperature. A little like his emotions, unstable, especially when the woman that holds his thoughts hostage is dressed in a black cocktail dress.

He spotted her far down the street. There was no big crowd to pick her out of but he was getting to know her walk, the soft bounce of her golden hair and the look of observation, of happiness and wonder in everything around her. He laughed a little at himself, of course she looks at everything like it is new, she just moved here. And that was a new dress for him to look at her in. Well maybe not new for her but for his eyes. A classic short black A line dress that swayed ever so slightly with each step she took. A silver shawl draped loosely over her shoulders leaving just enough to imagine the curves that lay beneath.

James cleared his head, a woman with a crying baby walked by jolting him back to his reality. No, he was not ready to go there again. Playing tour guide was an amusing distraction though. He smiled as Allie approached, "you appear to be ready for a little man hunting."

He was rewarded with an equally beaming smile and a twirl that rippled her skirt around her long legs. "Do you like it?" Allie asked genuinely curious.

"It will get the job done," he responded with a slight sneer. Which is is not quite what he intended, however to not make it not so noticeable he grabbed Allie's arm and twirled her to the door. "Just be prepared, all sorts of odd people show up to these things."

"Sounds like fun." The pair entered the bright open gallery. It was not a large space, the walls were bright creating an open feeling that allowed the eyes to focus on the art. In the center of the room were panels hanging down to form a square, the panel facing the entry had the word 'Torrid' in blue script letters across the top. Underneath was presumably one of the artist's paintings. Allie gave James a squeeze on the arm and walked forward. She wanted some time to wander and check out the artwork. She walked around the hanging panels and scanned the surrounding walls. All of the paintings were fairly similar, swirls of blues and greens with varying amounts of red.

She was standing near one painting when an arm came around her with a glass of champagne. She took the glass and had a sip of the sweet bubbly elixir. She figured it was James until she heard a higher pitched voice whisper in her ear. "Quick, don't think, tell me what you see."

"Squashed cockroaches," she responded quickly as instructed. The she flinched slightly. That was mostly what she had been thinking as she had been wandering around the room. She had no idea what the title Torrid was about, she was in no way an art critic or interpreter and, well, she did just say the first thing that came to mind.

When she turned around she was greeted by a stunned look on a flamboyant character. A sharp gasp with arms flailing as the artist turned and walked away caused Allie to take a much larger swig of her drink. Luckily a less zealous but better looking man was ready to step in. Allie turned to the tall blond, "I guess that was the artist," she said looking a little sheepish.

Tall blond guy laughed, "yes, don't worry about him though. I like your theory." He smiled as he gave an appreciative look that trailed down her body.

Allie gazed back just as conspicuously. Her new companion oozed confidence. And why shouldn't he Allie thought to herself. He was tall with broad shoulders, short blond hair which was sculpted into perfection. What really stood out was the intense green eyes that seemed to peer into one's soul. She held his gaze for several moments then turned back to the paintings. Her body was tingling, not only from the champagne but from the added attention. She could see a night out with this man in her future.

She glanced at him one more time, "not squashed bugs obviously," she thought for another moment but came up with nothing, "Then do they mean something or are they just a bunch of random swirls with red dots."

"Actually it is meant to be quite serious," he started with a matching tone. "It is the waters that rush in during a hurricane, the red represents the destruction left behind."

Allie looked at him a little quizzically, "is he referring to this past summer's hurricane? I am pretty sure it just skirted this area." She noticed a slightly offensive look forming on his face. "I mean, I am sure there was flooding and all but it was not that bad. Not quite like sitting in a hotel on the beach in Virginia watching as the waves got closer until they eventually breached the boardwalk. Sitting, hoping the large glass windows of the lobby held up to the winds." She drifted off remembering the debris hitting the windows.

His look softened, "sounds pretty intense, maybe you can tell me about it over drinks."

She smiled and was about to agree when a woman suddenly appeared between the two putting a literal freeze between them. "Jonathan," the woman nodded at her apparent acquaintance. She grabbed Allie by the elbow and pulled her aside. "Not him," she said in a low voice.

Just as suddenly James was by her side agreeing, "not him," he also said through gritted teeth.

Allie gave him a hard stare, "why not?" she mouthed back at him.

"He gets around too much, does not stick to one person, or one kind for that matter."

She looked back at the man that oozed hormones, weighing her options. She turned back, "maybe I am just looking for some fun anyway." She grabbed another glass of champagne from the waiter passing by.

"Suit yourself and don't say I did not warn you." James turned away. It was all he could do, she was an adult, capable of making her own decisions. Why should he care anyway? Because she was better than that, and deserved better. He shook his head, let her make her own mind up. He made a decision to not interfere any further. He had asked his friend Selena to watch out for Allie as well, perhaps she would do better without him there so he walked away and left the two of them alone.

"You must be James' new friend," the woman who first grabbed Allie's arm stated.

"Yes," Allie said mildly curious who this woman was.

"I am Selena, I own this gallery."

"Allie, nice to meet you," she said offering her hand and wondering if she and James had ever dated.

As if reading her mind Selena said, "James and I have been friends for a long time. He told me a bit about you. I am glad he has a new friend."

"We have been enjoying each other's company," Allie said not giving away any emotions.

"Good," she said, "what do you think of the show?"

"Interesting," she said slowly, "the art and the people."

"Welcome to New York honey." They both laughed. "Let me know if you need anything. As they say; any friend of James is a friend of mine."

Before Selena walked away Allie did have to know, "woman to woman, I should stay away from Jonathan?"

"From personal experience I am telling you to stay away."

Allie did not want details, she thanked her and went on her way. Apparently Jonathan had moved on, they were right about him. Another strikeout. She decided to study the artwork more although the more champagne she drank the more the blue swirls blurred together. She was feeling a little lightheaded, in a good way. She was able to mingle and meet all sorts of people. None quite as interesting as the man that asked her for a date. She did kept clear of James, though she did notice he was making his own way around the gallery conversing with his own groups. She wondered how many of them he knew, how many he was subtly steering away from her. Maybe he was doing her a favor. She let the last drops of her champagne hit her taste buds. Her own weekend was over and she was ready to head home. She found James to let him know she was leaving. She was not quite sure if she was thankful or mad at him, she would still give him the courtesy of not just disappearing.

"I will take you home," James immediately said.

Allie squinted her eyebrows at him, "I can manage by myself, thanks."

"I am going with you," he said with a little more conviction. "It is late, I don't want you to go by yourself."

"If you did not realize, I get home by myself every night after work."

James was quite aware, and he did not like it. This did not mean he had to let her go, especially in her apparent tipsy condition. "Well," he said taking the empty glass out of her hand, "presumably you are not drinking while working so don't make me walk ten steps behind you."

"Fine," Allie said with a slight roll of her eyes. She turned away from him and headed towards the door without checking to see how many paces behind her he was.

As they walked to the subway station Allie wobbled in her heels, James grabbed her arm to steady her. She turned and laughed, "that champagne was good."

"I am glad you had a good time."

"Selena seems pretty nice, ever date her?"

"No," James shook his head

"Why not, she is beautiful," Allie said recalling her long black hair and dark complexion. Then she remembered "oh well always surrounded by beauty you are." James did not respond, just focused on getting Allie home.

When they were situated on the train heading uptown, the effects of the champagne caught Allie off guard making her cold and tired. Her brain was still a bit fuzzy, looking for comfort she snuggled herself against James' arm and rested her head on his shoulder. She felt her body warm and relax, her eyelids slid down and her consciousness went to a quieter place.

James let her rest on him, her face was too peaceful to disturb. He was glad she did not protest him accompanying her, not that he considered himself her protector. She clearly needed help getting home otherwise she may end up somewhere in the Bronx at the end of the line. He glanced over at her smooth, soft skin and pulled her shawl up over her shoulders. So maybe he was protecting her. In a way that is what she asked for; to protect her from the weird ones, stalkers and users. Which is what was so confusing, giving her advice made her mad. He sighed, this was a no win situation.

He gently shook her awake just as they were pulling up to her station. She let out a big cat like stretch before rubbing her eyes open. She took in a big breath and looked at her escort. "Thanks for letting me sleep, I am good from here, you can just cross the track and take the next train downtown."

They stood and got out as the doors opened. "I don't mind walking you to your door."

Allie knew there would be no arguing, she gave him a half smile and headed towards the elevator that would take them to street level. Once outside they walked in silence for a short time, Allie had no particular comment about the evening.

James, though, wanted some clarity to her thinking. "So when you say you are just looking for some fun, are you really just looking for a one nighter? Because if that is the case," and he hoped not, "then I will stay clear."

Allie wrapped her shawl around herself a little tighter, she did not want an interrogation. "I meant what I said, I am looking to have fun. I could just start with a date, then what it turns into I will decide." Realizing that was not the answer he was looking for with the lack of response and gritted jaw she asked, "are you judging me?"

"I have no right to judge you," was his only response.

They had reached the door to Allie's apartment building and she could tell James was not happy. She was not insulted, she was happy he cared, it made her feel good. She turned to him and looked into his dark eyes. there was a warmth and comfort being so close to him. She took another step toward him, "you know," she started in a low soft voice while maintaining eye contact, "you could just date me and avoid this whole situation." She leaned in and gently held the back of his head with one hand. She closed her eyes and brushed his lips with hers. When he did not protest she inched even closer into his body and pressed her lips harder onto his sliding her tongue across just the outside taking in his taste.

James felt the shock from his lips right down to his core. He took in her sweet scent, tasting the last bit of champagne on her lips. He was completely under her control, he could not move, it was his body's wish to stay still and let her continue, let his body heat up and mold to hers. The sound of a honking taxi jolted him back to reality and he pulled back. It took a few breaths to get himself under control and partly cooled back down. There was hope in her eyes and he knew he would have to disappoint. Better to stop this now. He pushed her hair away from her face. "I am sorry, I just can't."

Allie knew that was a risky move, and even anticipated that response. Still she had to try and the champagne buzz was liquid courage. "All right James, I still had a fun night," she squeezed his hand, still feeling the warmth that now matched hers, still feeling a twinge of electricity. She watched him walk away silently. "Hey James," she called out to him. When he turned, she gave him a sultry smile, dropping her shoulder to allow her shawl to reveal her bare skin, "that was a really hot kiss."

Smoking hot, James thought to himself, a hot kiss from a hot woman that will drive him crazy. He could handle that, maybe, he thought. He softened his eyes and gave a slight nod and turned back.

"Hey James," Allie called one more time having a little fun with him. "Our deal still stands, helping me find a date."

Knowing that all was okay between them he smiled and nodded. "Good night," he said and walked away hoping she did not call him again. If she did he may not be able to keep moving. He picked up his pace until he heard the door close behind her when he then breathed in the cool night air to take his body temperature down.

Chapter 5

Allie sat at her desk trying to keep focused. The holiday parties were filling up the weekends, the party planners were constantly calling. The surveillance cameras had been installed and James was slated to check in that day. James, the person that kept her thoughts straying, kept her body constantly tingling. It has been almost forty eight hours since their kiss, they had not gotten together since, which despite her casualness about it was probably a good thing. She better find a distraction soon, preferably of the male persuasion that would take her mind off James.

Jenny entering her office would have to suffice for an immediate distraction. "Everything in place?" she asked Allie.

"Yes, and I left him instructions on where to leave the money. Hopefully we will catch the person this weekend and be done with it."

"Do you think it could be more than one person?"

"Sure, it is possible but we will watch and see what happens. In the meantime we just go about as if nothing is happening," she nodded her head to emphasize the importance.

"I know, anyway there is a young lady out in the lobby that says she knows you. Kelsey, with red hair?"

Allie had no problem remembering. "Oh yes, she is one of James' new models." They headed out to the lobby to find a very excited teenager. Allie went over to her and gave her a big hug. "Hey kiddo, it is great to see you."

"James said we should stay here, he said you were the manager and it is brand new and beautiful. He's right of course. Anyway I am here to do some more portfolio pictures and get some practice posing." She took a short breath and looked around, "I love this lobby, I feel like the tropics are right here in the city." She looked back at Allie, "so are you and James dating yet?"

Allie laughed at her and the directness only a young girl could have, "no."

"Well maybe I should have a talk with him about that," she said with her hands on her hips.

"No, that is not necessary, but thank you." She sat down with Kelsey on the couch and lowered her voice. "Did James tell you he was going to be here this weekend?" she asked thinking this may get a little sticky or she would have to hole up in her office for the next few days.

"Oh yes, he thought it would be great so that he could show me around and get to know me and my mom. He's so nice like that. I know my mom is still so worried about me doing this. I am so excited though, can you imagine, my picture in magazines!"

Allie smiled, she was excited and talked as teenagers do; non stop. She did have to get back to work so she grabbed Kelsey's hand. "Listen, James is actually here on a mission for me also. So this is good, he will look like a regular guest but I can not be hanging around you guys, it might look suspicious."

Kelsey's eyes widened, "of what?"

"Just a little employee issue, no worries though. You just need to enjoy your stay. If you need anything, let Jenny know, okay? She will take care of you."

"Okay, thanks."

As Allie looked up, James entered the lobby. She peeked a glance at his sleek self to keep in her memory for the next few days then scurried back to her office.

After two nights James reported that money went missing from his travel pouch. Well, not his travel pouch but one that Allie had supplied as bait. He followed Allie's instructions to report it to the front desk then Jenny passed it on. Allie spent her day reviewing staff schedules and videos. Every so often she would see James in the picture. She paused it when he was changing his shirt. She had let him know where the video was focused so he could have his privacy and that is why she generally only caught glimpses of him. She wondered if he was showing off to her knowing she would see it or if he was distracted by something else. She would never know, however she could take a minute to admire his sleek lines, his trim defined muscles without being overly buff. She traced her fingers across the video screen imagining how his skin would feel and how it would make her fingers tingle. If she ever got the chance. She sighed and pressed the fast forward button.

Allie never had to fire anyone before and she was feeling very agitated. She knew she was about to cut off someone's source of income and that she would not be able to give a letter of recommendation. The housekeeper did her job, was never late and seemed to get along with her coworkers according to her supervisor. She knew people became desperate but she made it clear her employees could go to her with any problems. She was anxiously waiting for her meeting and then she would be done for the day and the weekend.

When Sonya came in to see her she showed no signs that there was anything wrong. Allie did not want to make small talk, she needed to get straight to the point. After indicating for Sonya to have a seat she mentioned the three reports of stolen money.

Without flinching or even blinking Sonya said, "that is not good. I understand how this is a problem and I imagine you want to keep it quiet. Do you have any idea who did it?"

Allie tried to hide the actual reaction she wished to show. Though she should really not be shocked, Allie had enough work experience to know that someone could say that with an absolute straight face. In return Allie held her straight face gaze back. Not being a great investigator she decided to get straight to the evidence. She pulled up the video on her computer and turned the monitor. She cleared her throat while maintaining eye contact, "yes, in fact we do know who did it." She continued to watch Sonya's reaction as the video played. It was clear as day although it was very quick. In a matter of a few seconds she has the drawer open, the cash out of the wallet and stuffed in her pocket.

Sonya matched her swiftness with the briefest of reactions, a slight pinching of the eyebrows and clenching of the jaw before softening with a smile. "Well that is a nifty video trick."

Allie was getting angry, it was obvious she was caught and just as obvious she was not going to make this easy. "I assure you this is not a trick. I am the only one who has access to the videos," Allie responded with a little more determination in her voice, hoping it was not more like desperation.

Sonya mustered up more determination than Allie could. She stood up abruptly and dug her heels in. "You have nothing, you can not see anything in my hand. And what about the other two reports? I know you are new here, are you just trying to prove you are some sort of hot shot?"

Allie stood up, heart racing. Now that she was making it personal she knew for sure she had to be let go. "You have two options, leave your ID and access cards and walk away or I call the police. You are right, I have no evidence for the other two reports other than you did in fact clean those rooms on those days."

Only then did Sonya seem defeated which was only noticeable with a slight shift of her eyes. "I have mouths to feed you know."

"I know," Allie said holding her stance, there could be no softening or show of sympathy at this point, "you might think about that next time."

"I think about it all the time, you know for some people there is no so called American Dream, some of us will struggle for all of our lives, stuck in the same spot getting the same crappy pay," she waved her arm around indicating the crappy pay part included her current job. She started pacing back and forth with clenched fists.

Allie was not about to get into her personal history or the pay of an entry level position, she was ready for the meeting to end. She could see her employee's temper starting to flair. She was worried this was going to turn physical and needed to diffuse the situation. "Sonya, by all other standards you are a good employee. Don't ever think you could not have advanced within the company. Breaking the law is not the way to get there." She paused and the added, "I need a decision."

Sonya seemed to waver for a minute before tearing off her lanyard with her key cards. She threw them at Allie and stormed out the door.

Allie sat down drawing in a deep breath trying to steady her hands that she noticed were shaking. The meeting could have been much worse and there was no way to feel good about firing an employee. She did not presume it would get easier, hopefully it would not have to happen very often. With a weary sigh she started to enter her report.

Allie had slept in the last two mornings after the crazy weekend. She was missing her lunch dates and feeling a little lonely. While her general manager complimented her on handling the situation she did not feel much better. She was thankful when James called her to set up a lunch meeting. It was the only thing that would have gotten her out of bed that day.

A cup of coffee and a hot shower perked her up somewhat. The breeze was blowing lightly outside. The falling leaves and bare trees indicated the pending winter. Allie had no problem with jeans and sweater weather. While she liked the warm summers she also looked forward to the coolness of autumn. It was the perfect day to wander at South Street Seaport. It was another kind of tourist hot spot, another one that Allie wanted to learn about. At least it should be fairly quiet on a weekday.

She sent a message to James letting him know she was on her way. It would take a fair bit longer for her to get there.

She was getting used to the public transportation system and transferring subways and getting through the craziness of the crowds. It was after rush hour and the crowds were slightly diminished. Once on the train she did as most everyone else did and plugged in her ears and listened to music.

Allie had heard the seaport underwent a major transformation. She had seen images of the old style fish market, now what stood in its place was a huge glass structure. Apparently it was now a high end shopping mall. While she did want to see it for herself she was not sure how or even if lunch would come into play. There did not seem to be any food trucks around. Perhaps they would actually have a real sit down meal.

Or not. Allie saw James heading her way with a couple of what she assumed was wrapped sandwiches in one hand and two sodas in the other.

"Come on, let's find a bench by the water. I don't want these to get cold."

Allie followed him and they were lucky to find an empty bench. She could smell the sandwiches, "what do we have today?"

"Philly cheesesteaks. Hope you like the works."

"Absolutely." She bit into the thick pile of steak. She did her best to keep the peppers and cheese from oozing out.

James smiled as he watched Allie eat with a look of pure satisfaction on her face. He was considerate, he dug the extra napkins out of his pocket and handed them over before the drippings ruined her clothes. "Good stuff?"

Allie managed to nod. She finished chewing and asked, "where did you get them?"

"Food truck a few blocks away, Dave's, best cheesesteaks in the city."

After washing down his food with a final swig of his soda, James looked around and asked, "what do you think of all this?"

Allie wiped her mouth again, "I wish I got to see it before, seems the old fisherman style market was more quaint. Maybe the old no longer fits in here."

"I am all for progress, but I am not sure we need another glass shopping mall."

"Probably not. At least the view is nice." Allie could not come up with any other comment, not having been here when the change occurred. She watched a few ships go by then changed the subject.

"So how are things going with Kelsey?"

He nodded his head while he put his drink down. "Good, she signed on. Her mom will accompany her to any shoots. Usual stuff for a kid starting out."

"She must be excited." When she only got a slight nod in return she added, "and your bosses might leave you alone for a while." Again, another slight nod followed by another swig. "Are you all right James? You seem to be in a funk."

He shrugged his shoulders. "Everything is fine. Everyone is happy." He raised his can in cheers.

"Yeah, except you. What's going on?"

Why should he tell her he asked himself. It was not anyone's business anyway. She would likely be persistent though. Maybe telling someone with no prior knowledge would give him some relief. Not likely, even if she did tend to brighten his day. He knew she kept thinking it was work related, and in a round about way it was just not exactly the job itself. Oh well, what would it hurt to divulge a bit of information so she would let it go.

"Someone that was close to me passed away just about a year ago. Sometimes I will see something that triggers a memory. That's all. It will pass, nothing to be concerned about." Truly though, he hoped the memory would never pass even though it hurt a lot. A hurt he wanted to remember so he would not put himself in a position to have to go through it again.

"Sure I get that. That happened a lot after my father passed away. Still does on occasion. Now it does not hurt so much. Now I can smile at the memories."

Blah, blah, blah psycho babble talk was all he heard, yes trying to be helpful and all and without revealing details she could not know how deep the pain went. He politely smiled at her and changed the subject. "How about you? Tough weekend or did you find it exhilarating firing someone?"

"No, it was not enjoyable especially since she seemed like she wanted to beat the crap out of me."

"I am sure you could have taken her."

"Not likely, I just have a better evil eye and she backed down. Anyway I suppose the next time will be easier." She thought about him and what she was going. "I know I just got here but maybe it is time for a break. I should try being the guest for once and go away somewhere. Actually I have not taken a trip since college spring break. What about you, when was the last time you took a vacation?"

"I travel a lot for work."

"That is not quite the same thing."

"I am not concerned about me," James commented. "But give me a day, maybe I can help you out. I have to get back to the office."

Allie watched him go, she planned on walking around more. She was glad James finally shared a small part of himself. It was not much. She would take it and keep putting small pieces of his life together. She was looking forward to seeing what he had in mind.

The next day Allie's inbox was bombarded with emails from James. She smiled as she read each one. James was taking Kelsey to St. Thomas for a photo shoot. The rest of the messages were basically: Please you have to come, No You Must come, Please, I will pay. then in tiny letters: will have to share a room, will make sure there are two beds(smiley face). Then again in big letters: Remember, This Is For You! Allie only half believed that, she decided to pick up her phone.

"What is wrong, you can't handle a sixteen year old and her mother?"

"Of course I can, it is my job." He paused for a moment, "but she will talk my ear off. Anyway she loves you. It will help her relax, she is still a little unsure of herself in front of the camera."

"And sharing a room?"

"You can try booking one if you want, just trying to help out." James figured he would be working anyway and would not be spending that much time in the room. Besides they were adults, they could handle it, he tried to convince himself.

"No, it is fine, no problem here. I will switch my Sunday shift and we will be all set to go. And thanks, James."

"I will send you the details," he said before hanging up. He sighed, he was not sure what he was getting himself into. He was not sure how he even agreed to take a beautiful woman to the Caribbean. Not that it was the first time. He shook his head trying to rid whatever was controlling the subconscious part of his brain. He finished up some work at his desk and decided to call it quits for the day. He told Cheryl to go ahead and book a ticket for Allie.

His somewhat overprotective and nosy secretary suddenly lit up, "she agreed to go?"

"Yes," he said turning back, eyeing his employee warily.

"You know honey, if you don't scoop her up someone else will."

He stepped closer to her desk, "you don't even know her, what makes you think I am even interested?"

"I know that look," she winked at him.

"What look?" he asked knowing the answer, hoping she would have a different one.

"Twitter-patted darling," she smiled turning her attention back to her computer.

James turned in a huff, this was not a fairytale, this was real life. And in real life people got hurt, no more for him. He sure hoped someone would scoop her up.

Chapter 6

Allie breathed a sigh of relief when the plane leveled out. The day was overcast with a brisk wind bouncing the plane as it passed above the grey clouds. Not that she was too worried but there is always that one moment that makes you think twice when you feel yourself drop in your seat before being pushed back up. She had flown a few times in her life but not often enough to be completely relaxed. She glanced briefly at James, he was sitting in the window seat, she did not want to see how high they were flying. His eyes were closed with his hands clasped on his lap. She wondered how many times he had been in that same seat flying across the world. She took a closer look watching his eyes in rem motion beneath his dark eyelids. Subconsciously his arms moved across his chest and his breathing became more rapid. It made her desire to know what was troubling him even stronger. And more than that she wanted to reach over and softly press her lips on his restless eyes and kiss them back to sleep. Before her own breath could get too rapid she settled for squeezing his arm to see if he wanted a drink from the passing flight attendants.

She passed his cup of coffee and placed her orange juice on the tray in front of her. She normally would be drinking coffee but she did not feel like she needed anymore caffeine nor did she have any desire to need to use the tiny bathrooms.

"How was your catnap? I am surprised you slept thought that take off." There had been a delay on the tarmac so Allie did understand how James did fall asleep. She had been busy watching the safety video when she realized he seemed to be drifting off.

He took a sip of his coffee and sunk back into his seat. "Sorry about that, long night working out the logistics. And Kelsey," he let out a rare chuckle, "texting me all night. She is very excited you are going by the way."

Allie smiled at that, she liked Kelsey. "It's nice of you to respond to her texts."

"Well, she is just a kid, her parents seem nice but sometimes teens need someone else to talk to."

"Do you ever work with younger kids?"

"No," he replied very quickly. "The youngest I will go is fourteen and they are hard enough to keep straight. Plus the parents, I wish I could keep them out of the picture all together, but that would be illegal," he added sarcastically.

"Or unethical?" Allie added

"Probably," he grumbled.

"Well, you know my kids are going to be the smartest, most beautiful and talented kids out there," Allie said while flipping her hair knowing it would irk him. After a quick evil eye in response they both laughed.

James appreciated the light moment. The next few days would be fairly busy and he was hoping Allie would be able to occupy herself and not hang around him too much. Besides not having time and not wanting to explain everything going on he also did not think he could handle seeing her in sundresses or bikinis or whatever else she brought. Even her hair flipping was enough distraction. She was good company though, he focused on the dream he had during takeoff and let his feeling for her quickly vanish. Remembering his anger and disappointment helped keep him in check. Yet he could not dwell on it either. He finished his coffee and refocused on the upcoming trip. "I made a dinner reservation tonight with Kelsey and her mom, I hope you will come too," he said thinking Kelsey would be thrilled. And she was the distraction he would use to keep Allie occupied.

"Of course," she said lightly, what else would she do she thought to herself.

"They will be arriving about an hour after us."

"Sounds good," she paused then added, "thanks for bringing me James."

He nodded slightly but had to look away before her beautiful smile started melting and cracking the ice around his heart.

The warm tropical breeze sent Allie's hair around her shoulders and flying off to her side. She lifted her head to the sky taking in the warm sun. She was waiting just outside the cover of the open air reception area waiting for James' models to arrive. Besides Kelsey he had two others on the way. Being more seasoned he was less worried about them than the young one that had never before been on a location shoot. And Allie really was only worried about Kelsey not being too nervous. Otherwise her only goals for the next few days were to enjoy a few drinks, swim in the ocean, watch the palm trees swaying in the breeze and soak up the warm salty air. Allie took another sip of her Mai Tai and turned around with a smile when she heard Kelsey's excited voice.

"OMG, is this not the coolest place you have ever seen?" She was mostly skipping around, touching all the potted palms, sitting in the wicker furniture, twirling across the terra cotta floors. Then she screeched Allie's name in a long drawn out song, "I am so glad you are here." She ran over and hugged her new friend.

"It is beautiful," Allie agreed, "how are you feeling? A little nervous?"

Her eyes and smile only shifted for a millisecond, "no, it's exciting," she said with her smile returning. The pair stood hand in hand for a few more minutes taking in the views of the pool and inviting waters of the Caribbean and beyond. The resort was broken up into several small building on either side of the pool and restaurants. They all had oceanfront balconies or patios. The white sand beach stretched all the way across the resort property with palms dotting the landscape. Hammocks hung amongst the trees and loungers and palm umbrellas took up the the open unshaded spaces.

It was an all inclusive resort which Allie planned to take full advantage of, with the plan to never be without a tropical drink in hand. She was ready to be out on the beach. She and James had already checked into their room and declared beds and drawer space. Allie did not plan on spending too much time in there.

She turned when she felt Kelsey's grip on her hand tighten and she realized she heard the clacking of high heels on the floor. She saw James speaking to two of the most beautiful women she had ever seen. Then she realized

Kelsey was probably thinking the same thing and feeling out of place. She turned to face the suddenly down stricken teenager. "Hey, James would not have brought you here if he did think you belonged."

Kelsey pursed her lips in thought for a moment, "but I can not compete with them," she said with a very slight whine to her voice.

"This is not a competition honey."

"Modeling is always a competition," she responded with a little too much maturity.

"Listen to me, you are right in a way, you will always be competing for contracts. You are young and beautiful and we don't know what they are looking for. This will be a great experience for you. I can tell you most girls do not jump right to something like this. So no matter what happens enjoy the view and learn what you can. And most of all be yourself and trust James." Allie had no real experience and basis for her advice but she was sure they could trust him.

Kelsey relaxed and closed her eyes letting the smile return, "you're right. See you for dinner?" she asked as her mother came over with the key cards to their room.

Being that dinner was only a short time away, Allie decided the beach was not worth having to shower and change two more times. Instead she wandered over to the bar to refill her drink. Not that she planned on being a total lush through her stay but a light buzz would do her good. She still needed to maintain her self control with James though. So far she had only seen women strolling around with 5th avenue outfits. There was an odd lack of men at the resort and wondered what it meant. Oh well, the beach would have to be enough. Watching the news updates on the bar tv was not her idea of a break from life. The soccer games were about as boring as watching a tennis match to her as well. Allie took a bigger swig of her drink and almost spit it out when the hand on her shoulder made her jump.

She was ready to push James for making her do that but then realized it was not him. Standing before her was a very tall man who looked like he belonged on a California beach with a surf board. He was tan with medium length sandy hair that was pushed back as if he had just jumped out of the water. His cutoff shorts and tank top showed off his well muscled tan arms and legs. Allie, already feeling the light buzz from her two drinks thought she could definitely drink him as well. She looked at him as if she was studying a scientific object. "So there are male specimens at this resort," she said to him matter of fact.

He looked slightly puzzled then let out a slight laugh as he went along with her story, "will there not be another sample joining you?"

"No," she responded, "however, I am always in search of new exotic samples to study." She made a point of eyeballing him from the top of his head all the way down to his flip flopped feet. Why not she thought to herself, men do it to women all the time. Besides she felt a little like the Vegas commercial at the moment. What happened in the Caribbean would stay in the Caribbean.

"Well then, I may be interested in volunteering myself, all in the name of scientific research of course," he smiled as he pulled up the stool next to Allie.

Allie was having fun with this but she did not want to come across that easy, even if she was more than willing at the moment. She would have to slow down on the tropical drinks just a touch. "I think with a little preliminary research I will let you know if you will be accepted into my full study."

He cocked his head and asked, "and how many specimens do you research at one time?"

"Ah, well I like to give my full undivided attention to one specimen a a time."

Her new companion ordered himself a beer and took a long swig. He was quite good looking she thought and she was definitely leading him on, and she was rather okay with that. "Allie, by the way, so are you here for business or pleasure?"

"Sean," he said and after a moment of thought added, "at this moment: pleasure."

"Well then," she took one of his hands in both of hers rubbing her thumbs across his palms, "I look forward to starting my research, however, for this evening I have promised dinner to friends." She took a few steps before turning back, "perhaps dinner tomorrow? Around 7?"

"It will not be an easy wait," he said with eyes glued on her as she walked away.

Dinner was a lot of chatter about schedules and finding out who was doing hair and makeup. Allie was trying to seem interested and pay attention to the conversation. Sean was on her mind and she kept trying to peek around looking for him. He was not really clear on why he was at the resort, not that it mattered. It was possible he could have been part of this group, she did not think so though. She looked over at James concentrating on the meeting. He was being really patient with Kelsey's mother and her perpetual questions. It was another quality that he probably did not think much of and she took notice of. Allie looked away not wanting to overthink the situation. Sean would provide a nice distraction for now and helping Kelsey was on her agenda as well.

Kelsey was sitting between Allie and James with Kelsey's mother sitting on the other side of James. She had a notebook in hand, writing down everything that was being said, which let Kelsey spend the same amount of time on her phone. Allie smiled to herself, while she should be paying a little more attention she was sure Kelsey's mother would not let her miss a beat.

Allie leaned over and whispered in Kelsey's ear, "have a boyfriend back home you are texting?"

"What?" she said suddenly looking up, "me? No, I don't have a boyfriend. This is my friend Gracie." Kelsey got serious for a moment. "She has cancer, her hair started falling out so she thinks she looks ugly, which is most definitely not true. Seriously she should be here. Anyway she is really sick and sometimes I feel bad telling her about being here but she insists I tell her all the details."

"You are a good friend, besides she needs to see happiness, a reason to keep fighting. Do you have a picture of her?"

Kelsey handed over her phone after swiping through her photos. Allie looked at a picture of a girl that had more spark in her eyes than anyone she knew. While she had a look of exhaustion and pain, her eyes were full of life and hope. "She is beautiful, what do you think James?" she asked him as she handed over the phone.

He looked over, seemingly thrown off guard. He paused his conversation and studied the phone. He handed the phone back with a smile, "she has great bone structure and symmetrical features. Her eyes, well they certainly can tell a story."

Kelsey took the phone and shrugged, "I will tell her what you said but she won't agree." She pointed to her head, "she hates that all her hair fell out."

It only took a brief moment for a spark to light in Allie's head, "hey James have you ever done photo shoots with kids with cancer?

"What?" he said slightly confused, "oh no, um, I had not really thought about it."

"Oh yes," Kelsey said giddily, "Gracie would love it, show her she is still beautiful. Can we James?"

"Um, I am not sure," he said looking a little disturbed.

"Don't worry," Allie whispered to Kelsey, "I will work on him."

Allie was sitting back in the room flipping though the local brochures even though she had no intention of going anywhere besides the beach. Perhaps she would come back in the future and venture out, for now though it was strictly r and r. After dinner the party had split up, James was still talking business. Kelsey had gone back to her room, dragged by her mother insisting she needed to sleep. That left Allie two choices: go back to the bar or back to the room. She felt she drank enough and was feeling a little tired from the overall day of traveling and socializing.

Truly though, she wanted to be there when James came back, she wanted to explore the idea of going to see sick kids and helping them feel good about themselves. And maybe it would help James get out of his funk. Or make it feel like he was putting his skills to good use. She did not consider herself a major fashionista, still she did not think it would take too much to make girls feel pretty again. She reached over to the notepad on the nightstand and began a list of things she thought they might need.

Thirty minutes later and only a short list accomplished, Allie heard the key card slide in the lock. James came in the room, kicked off his shoes and threw the key card on the dresser. He dashed into the bathroom before Allie could say anything.

James had been hoping Allie would not be in the room or at least asleep. He knew he would have to be up and out early so he would be able to avoid her in the morning. He had hung around with some of the crew for the shoot, he did not need to he just did not want to talk about her idea. He had no interest in talking to sick kids. He was already struggling with being on the verge on his own depression. Now he was supposed to make friends with sick kids and watch them die? Forget that, he would not do it. He threw on his tee shirt and quickly jumped into his own bed. He reached over to turn off the light. "Before you say anything, the answer is no, I am not doing it."

Allie looked at him, not understanding the complete unwillingness, "can't we at least talk about it?"

"No," he said a little too forcefully, he turned over officially ending the conversation.

The next evening Allie was getting ready for dinner, she was not sure if Sean would remember or not. It really did not matter to her either way although the company would be nice. She had spent the day mostly by the pool soaking up the sun and sipping a variety of fruity drinks. Occasionally she dropped herself into the pool to cool off. Lunch was brought to her side by a young handsome waiter.

She was not sure where all the crew from the fashion shoot had gone. By afternoon she had assumed it was too hot and the light of the sun would be too strong. Perhaps they had gone to some other part of the island, she was not sure and not very interested. She was sure Kelsey would fill her in at some point.

She tried not to think too much of James, she was not going to give up though. At least not until he gave her a good reason. Either way she was would figure out a way to go forward with the idea and hope that James would be on board eventually. She took one last look at herself in the mirror. She was wearing a simple halter style sun dress and cloth strap sandals. Smiling, she headed to what she hoped would be a very nice evening.

Allie had not specified at which restaurant they should meet. There were only three to choose from but two of them required reservations which she did not make. Leaving only one as the likely option she headed over to the open seating buffet area. The menu changed nightly, she was looking over the display board when the hairs on the back of her neck stood up. Her hair had been pushed aside, words whispered in her ear, words she did not decipher. Despite finishing her last cocktail several hours ago, her whole body was once again buzzed in giddiness. A strong hand turned her around and led her away. She had to focus on walking, the tingling spreading from her fingertips up her arm was fogging her brain. It had been too long since she allowed herself the touch of man and her body was telling her it was ready.

Allie barely heard the words reservations for two, somehow she managed to follow the hostess to a quiet beachside table. Finally her brain started to tune back in when she heard Sean say, "I thought this might be a little nicer, more private," he added with a slight smile.

"Ah yes, perfect for my studies," she replied back continuing their little role playing from the previous night.

He held the chair out for her which she appreciated just as much as she appreciated how he looked. Wearing linen pants, a button down silk shirt and sandals, he exuded the ideal beach resort patron. His sandy hair and sun bronzed complexion completed the picture. "And so far," she said as she sat down placing her napkin on her lap, "I like what I see."

Allie did not want to delve into reality just yet, she had no idea where Sean was from. Assuming she would not see him again after she left she just wanted to enjoy his company. They made light teasing conversation. She held onto her role as scientist, touching varying parts of his body. She commented on his soft ear lobes, strong jaw line, slightly roughened elbows and hands. She held the gaze of his green eyes while her hands wandered down to his fingertips. She knew she was daring him to take her back to his room, hers would not be an option. Perhaps she was being a little unfair not knowing if she would take him up on it if offered. She just could not help herself. She had to have so much restraint with James, with Sean though, she made no effort to hold back.

After dinner, they walked over to the bar to pick up another round of drinks to take over to the beach. Allie stood at the edge of the outdoor patio taking in the scene while waiting for Sean. The sun had already set, the night air was still warm and the moon was shining bright. A soft breeze coming off the ocean ruffled the palm trees. She was relishing in her dream like state when a hardened voice brought her back to reality.

"Am I to assume you will not be returning to the room this evening?" James asked through pursed lips.

Allie stared right back, "I don't think you should be assuming anything. Besides why would you care what I do?"

"I don't," he replied gruffly shrugging his shoulders. "Just wanted to know if I should be expecting you back, that is all."

"I will tell you what, I will send you a text if I am not coming back, okay?"

"Fine," he answered, he turned and with a nod to Allie's date, Sean, "don't mess with her." Without looking back at her, he walked away.

Shit, Allie thought to herself, she was sobering up way too quickly. Was it really possible they knew each other?

Sean seemed to be having the same reaction. "Please don't tell me you are here with James," he said handing her another frozen concoction.

There was no getting out of this one, she just needed to spin it in the right way. She took a deep breath, "okay, yes I am here with James. But not in the way you think. I am just tagging along."

Allie noticed him working his jaw, deciding whether or not to believe her. He did not comment right away, just took her hand and led her down to the waters edge. Sean sat down on one of the lounge chairs and motioned for Allie to sit with him. He had each leg hanging off either side of the chair and she sat sideways in between. He had let go of her hand so she sat twirling the stirrer in her drink while she watched the moonlit waves lap softly on the sand. There was obviously history between the two of them which should have nothing to do with her.

The silence was ridiculous especially after the fun dinner they had. She turned and waited for him to finish his swig from the beer he was downing. "James and I met by chance. He was asked to judge a model contest, which I am sure you know he never does. Anyway I happened to be hanging around, he looked bored, I made him laugh. I was and am still new to the city so I was looking for a friend. We hang out, have lunch, he shows me around. That is it," she added more pronounced.

He sat closer to Allie searching her eyes, "no further interest in him beyond just friends?"

Obviously he would see through her if she denied it, she could not hold his stare, "it really does not matter, James made it clear he is not interested."

"Hmm, I would not be too sure of that."

Allie was not sure how to take that and the evening was going downhill. Still maybe she could get some insight out of him and maybe set things straight. "Even if that was true whatever put him into his no dating funk, he is not over it yet. I can't get him out of it. And I don't mean seducing him out of it. Last night Kelsey and I had an idea to do some glamour shots for sick kids, we thought that might make him feel good."

"Forget that, he will never agree," Sean said interrupting her.

"Why do you say that?"

"Did he ever tell you what happened about a year ago?"

"No, I figured he would tell me when he was ready."

"He will probably not like this but I am going to tell you anyway. His last girlfriend, a model, did not show up for a shoot one day. They had been dating for about a year, that was pretty long for him. They seemed happy together, having lots of fun." He finished off his beer in one last long swig. "He found out that day from one of her friends that she was at an abortion clinic. He was pissed, he left running; cursing and ranting."

"He was too late wasn't he?" Allie asked quietly.

"Yup, never forgave her. He would have married her. She was worried about gaining weight and losing contracts."

"Thanks for telling me," there was no other way to respond. And it would not change her relationship with James. And she was still sitting next to an incredibly sexy man. "So did you and James often compete for the same woman?"

He smirked before he answered, "sometimes."

"And he won the most."

"He did."

"Let's see, James is here for a photo shoot, you are here and you know each other, that means you are the...?" She looked at him head tilted waiting for him to finish.

"The photographer," he answered as if an understatement.

"0f course." Allie could not believe the position she was in. What were the chances this would happen. Not so slim she supposed since they were there for the same reason. She figured she had two choices: hang out by herself the rest of the trip or try to have fun with Sean. Since there seemed to be few other guys hanging around she decided on option two. "Well perhaps the tide is turning."

"Perhaps," he said running his hand through Allie's hair. "Come on, I will walk you back to your room."

Allie felt her happy bubble bursting just as it had with every other guy that showed an interest in her when James was involved. Not that it should matter, a few nights on an island did not mean much. It just felt so good to have a man so near her, pay attention to her, make her skin tingle. She picked up Sean's hand and laced her fingers in his. She wanted to keep her interest in him known. She smiled to herself when he rubbed his thumb along her hand. Maybe he was doing it out of habit she thought noting that he was looking off into the distance, at least he had not let go. When they reached her door she squeezed his hand and pulled him to face her. "Sean, James made it clear he was not interested in dating. And I like you." She ran her other hand up his chest then across his cheek.

Sean took a second with closed eyes, then he took a deep breath, looked into Allie's eyes with a smile He reached down and softly brushed his lips across hers. "Come down to the beach at sunrise and watch the shoot."

"I will be there. And you will be the one behind the camera".

Allie did a quick pose as he pretended to take a photo of her before turning away. He was handsome, suave, slightly cocky and in competition with the agent. She could not quite believe she was now caught in between the two of them. Of all the beautiful people they were both around and somehow they picked her. Well not really James, or at least that was what she needed to convince herself.

She closed the door softly behind her thinking James would be asleep, not sure if that was what she was hoping. Seeing him sitting outside she needed to decide whether or not to let him know she knew his past or pretend she did not have the conversation with Sean. She looked at him from across the room twirling the ceramic mug with his finger staring in the dark distance at likely nothing in particular. He looked sullen slumped in his seat, bare feet crossed. She was not sure what the right decision was, she could not ignore him though.

After sliding the door closed, Allie sat down but did not make an effort to start a conversation. Either he would choose to talk or not, she never pushed him before and she would not start now.

A few awkward silent moments later James finally did speak, "I did not think you would be back tonight, or was it a quickie and you are done with him?"

Allie shook her head, she did not have to sit here with him being nasty. She was not going to try to talk to him now. She got up and turned to go back inside when a hand grabbed her and brought her back around.

"I am sorry," James said quietly. "I should not have said that, it is none of my business anyway."

"Nothing happened, Sean seems to think this may be another competition between the two of you, he thinks..."

"Yeah, Elsa picked me," he quickly interrupted. "Along with one or two others, but he won sometimes too." He went from using his finger to twirl the mug to his whole hand causing the whole table to vibrate. He felt Allie's hand clamp down on his, he really wanted to fling the mug off the balcony and hear it smash on the sidewalk below. Instead the soft warmth of Allie's hand took him off guard. He could feel himself starting to shake slightly, not enough for anyone else to notice, just enough for him. He did not like the feeling, he did not have to share his feelings. What good would it do anyway, he wondered. That was for women, yet this woman sitting here made him want to do just that. And somehow she made him want to talk without egging him on, without asking any questions, just a soft touch from her hand. He pulled his hand away and crossed his arms.

"Do you know what it was like? First it was every pregnant woman I saw, I don't know how far along she was but I guessed around eight weeks. I imagined what she would look like at three then four months, then being able to find out if it was a boy or a girl. She would have been beautiful and I would have married her."

"James, you are torturing yourself," Allie said with a true look of concern on her face.

"It gets worse, after around the time the baby would have been born then I noticed every newborn and again what my baby look like. Allie, that was my baby too. I know I had no right over what she did with her body but there was a life in there that I created too."

Allie was taken aback by his passion, she really had no immediate response, there was nothing that would make it better. Maybe she could help him move forward. "Why is it that you are shutting yourself out from women if you want to be a father?"

He shrugged off the question, "there are other ways to have kids."

"You are so thick headed," she grumbled back at him. "Fine, write off women then but not kids, they love you and you can do a lot of good." Allie got up, she would always be there for him to talk, He was shutting down though and that was okay. What he revealed was more then she expected. She turned back to him and just gave him a smile and nod of thanks, no words necessary at this point.

"What do the boys get?" Allie heard him ask just as she was to close the patio door.

"What?" she asked confused by the change of conversation.

"If the girls get princess makeovers what do the boys get?"

Allie was trying hard to hide her excitement that he had actually been thinking of her idea. "Hmm, pirates?"

"Superheroes, I think."

"I like it," she smiled one last time and went inside.

Allie woke up the next morning feeling that the day would somehow be a turning point. She did not know which direction it would go, she did not want to think of the consequences of either. She would only gain in the situation and she would not influence fate.

James had already left and even though she did plan on heading to the beach to watch the photoshoot she did not have to be there before the sun broke the horizon. She stretched and crawled out of bed and happily poured a cup of coffee that James had left brewing. She pulled aside the window curtains to let what little bit of light there was to filter in the room. Working nights meant late mornings for her although the view of the pink sky with the tall slightly bent coconut palms made it worth getting up early. Plus she had promised Kelsey she would be there. It would be her first official shoot and Allie was hoping she would not be too nervous.

There was a slight breeze blowing giving a slight crispness to the morning air. Fully expecting the temperature to change to full out heat Allie went ahead and put on her two piece suit with long cotton flowing pants and matching cotton hooded cover up. So what that they were slightly shear showing off the turquoise bikini she was wearing, it was still the beach and she was still on the hunt.

By the time she reached the beach a short time later, she had minimized the makeup and pulled her hair into a pony tail, a few clouds were streaking across the sky adding brilliant bands of pinks and oranges to the waking horizon. She saw James first, he looked frustrated standing with his arms across his chest. The whole scene seemed to be stop motion. There were tents that likely had hair and makeup in progress. There were lights and screens that were waiting to be adjusted. And there was a variety of people sitting in directors chairs waiting for something to happen. Allie thought the whole thing was odd especially with the ever changing light. She strolled over to James, it was a new day with no plan to mention the previous evening's conversation. She lightly squeezed his arm to get his attention. "Good morning," she said as cheerfully as she could for the early hour.

"Hey," he said without looking. He shoved his hands in his pockets and looked down. He was grateful to Sean for telling her the truth. He should have asked first but it was difficult for him to talk about. Of course Allie was completely understanding and mostly supportive. It did not change his attitude towards relationships. He did decide to take his focus off what his child might look like. Allie was right, he was torturing himself and he was making himself miserable. He could not change what happened and he could not drag himself down anymore. What else he would do for himself he had yet to decide. He did know of one thing he had to do right at that moment before he lost his nerve.

He turned and looked at the person that somehow made her way into his life, making him see how he had a chance to find some sense of happiness again. And despite this he needed to let her go, let her live. Let her have fun even if it meant risking their friendship. Ultimately he would drag her down, he would not be able change in an instant, forget everything all at once. Of course when he turned to look at Allie he almost threw all that out the window, or into the ocean in this case. Did the outfit have to be see through? Was she trying a new way to torture him? He refocused and shook off his wavering feelings. "Sean is a good guy, you should go be with him."

Allie looked into his eyes, trying to her hide her own disappointment. He would not, or maybe could not, hold her gaze. That was fine, she thought to herself, he obviously was still not ready and she would not be one of those women who sat around waiting for something that may never happen.

She smiled releasing the tension in her shoulders, "so you are going to let Sean win this round?" She suddenly felt bad after she said that since he just looked down and shrugged his shoulders. Allie ran her hand quickly through his hair and gave him a hug, "we can still have lunch, right?"

"Of course, and don't mess with the hair," he answered lightening the atmosphere while he finger combed his hair back in place. "Hey listen, Kelsey needs help loosening up down there, I can't seem to get through to her, I think her mother is making it worse."

Allie looked back down to the beach and saw Kelsey standing head down looking defeated. She definitely had to help. "I will see what I can do." She started walking away but looked back briefly, "James, I don't think I will be back in the room tonight." She gave a wink and a smile before continuing on her path.

First, there was something else she needed to do. She went up to the photographer and combed one hand through his sandy hair and held his cheek with the other. As tall as she was, she still had to reach up to meet his soft lips. She wanted to give him a small taste to keep him thinking of her throughout the day. Allie was not sure if he still wanted to see her, she wanted to find out though. She pressed her lips to his, not asking for much but she did steal a quick taste of him. He did not offer more, he also did not pull back, she looked up into his green eyes, "good morning handsome."

Sean reached down and picked up Allie's hand. "So you choose me?" he asked her, head tilted.

Allie knew from the serious expression on his face that she had to think quickly and answer carefully. Technically he was her only choice but she did not think that was what he was looking for. "Sean, I like you and I want to get to know you."

"I'm sorry, it is not important, let's have dinner tonight."

She breathed a slight sigh of relief and smiled when she caught his eyes grazing over her. If he kept it up she would have to throw her heated up body in the ocean. In an effort to regain her focus Allie turned her attention back to Kelsey to see how she was doing. She looked like she was ready to break into tears. She felt Sean's breath on the back of her neck, "please go do something with her, we already lost the best light but we may be able to get a few good shots."

Allie trotted down to the water's edge. Kelsey was circling her toes in the sand letting the softly lapping waves wash out her lines. Her two piece white embroidered bathing suit revealed a young woman's body, her face though, revealed a scared teenager.

Allie watched as Kelsey's mother sighed heavily, "I told her we could go home, that she did not have to do this."

Allie was glad she was not being the pushy mother forcing her daughter to do something she did want to or was not ready for. Based on the fact that Kelsey was not moving she figured the young model just needed a nudge in the right direction. "Of course, I am sure she appreciates not feeling pressured," she said and waited for mom to step aside.

"Hey sweetie," she said taking both her hands in hers.

Holding back a sniffle Kelsey asked, "will you be mad at me if I can not do this?"

"Of course not." And she would not, she did want her to relax though. She wiggled her arms and started slowly spinning in a small circle with her. She did not mind that the water was soaking the bottom of her pants. "The water feels good," she said splashing some on Kelsey's legs. That almost got a smile out of her. "You know you look incredible in this suit." Her skin was glowing and the sun was picking up the red and blond streaks in her hair. Allie did not relay that though, she was sure someone had already told her.

"It is pretty isn't it?" she replied with a sheepish smile.

Allie leaned in and whispered in her ear, "you look sexy hot, you do know that don't you?"

That got an even bigger response as she pushed her hair to the side tilting her chin to the sky. She finally looked at Allie and smiled, "you look pretty good yourself, I saw you kiss Sean."

Allie led Kelsey a little ways down the beach swinging her hand and kicking at the water. "What do you think, kind of cute right?"

"Oh yeah," she said with the most enthusiasm Allie had heard from her all morning. "What about James though, I thought you liked him."

"Let's just say the timing is not right." She did not want to go into details so she turned the tables. "what about you? Any lucky guy for you?"

"No, nothing official anyway."

Allie knew this was the key, she turned them around and started back to where the water was lapping against the big rocks where they had first stood. "So what is his name, what does he look like, does he play sports?" she tried to make herself sound like an excited teenager.

She was rewarded with a laugh and a smile. "His name is Logan, he is an amazing baseball player. And he plays the drums. He knows he is cute and popular but he is so nice to everyone."

"Does he know you are here looking like this?" she pointed at her. Allie finally let go of Kelsey's hand and backed away sitting on the small boulder in the water.

Kelsey shrugged her shoulders, "yeah he knows. I think he feels I am going to be jetting around the world hanging out with male models and forget all about him."

"Well then I think we will have to take a picture of you and send him a wish you were here note." Allie saw her blush, she knew what he would be going through. Potentially dating someone who had access to all these beautiful models was not going to be easy. They could talk about that later though, for now she had to get her friend posing for the camera. "Do you trust me?"

"Yeah, why?" she asked curiously.

"Pretend you are at home, house to yourself. You are in your room trying on your summer clothes; sundresses, bikinis, whatever. There is a picture of Logan on your phone. He is not there, you are just pretending he is sitting on your bed watching. You are letting him know you want him, and there is no one there so let loose, what would you do if no one was watching?"

Allie watched as Kelsey started walking in circles, she cupped some water in her hand and poured it down her front. Slowly she transformed from awkward teenager to sexy young adult. She subtly shifted her expressions as she ran her hands through her hair and down her sides. She kneeled down into the water and continued the show. It was a good thing Logan was not there. Allie took a quick peek to the side and was pleased to see Sean shooting away. James was there also looking pleased. She thought Kelsey was doing a good job, she hoped they thought so also.

She went back to watching. She did not want to keep looking at James and Sean standing next to each other. She knew they often crossed paths, personally and in work She did not know if it would be possible to keep both of them in her life, she was not willing to let James go completely. Hopefully Sean would be okay with that. If not, well she was getting ahead of herself anyway.

A loud humming noise brought her attention back. She turned just in time to see a jet ski whizzing by along with a wave that came washing over her and Kelsey. Not having time to react the force knocked her into the sand and water. She was laughing when she sat up, then another wave threw her back off balance. Kelsey started laughing also, her hair was plastered to her face, makeup starting to run. Finally able to stand, Allie flipped her hair back and helped Kelsey up out of the water. Several members of the crew were heading their way, James and Sean stayed in place completely amused by the whole situation.

They walked to the dry sand and wrapped towels around themselves. Allie looked over, "you were really good, Logan would have melted right into the sand." She actually thought the wave was perfect timing, Kelsey was getting a little too sexy. She was still only a teenager.

"Really?" she asked, "I mean, it felt really good, I just let myself dream and go with it."

"That's good, why don't we see what the experts think." Sean and James were still laughing when they reached them.

Sean stopped fairly quickly when he realized Allie's clothes were now completely see through revealing her soft curves. He regrettably pried his eyes away in the attempt to stay professional. Instead he looked at the young lady, "that was great, I think we got what we needed."

"You liked it?" she asked with a beaming smile.

James jumped in, "he would not say that if it was not true, trust me, he does not waste his time."

Kelsey took a step back, "thanks for being patient then."

"Everyone new deserves a chance, come on let's go over to the the tent and take a look."

"Thanks for the help," James said, "I don't think she would have been able to do it without you here."

Allie ran her hand through her wet hair, "sure, she is a great kid. Catch up with you later," she left them to do their work and headed back to the room to change.

By the time Allie had gone to switch beachwear and returned to the sand the model shoot from the morning had been dismantled. The sun was high and bright and the day was heating up. Even the ocean breeze could not take much of the edge off the climbing temperature. She dropped her beach bag and water at one of the shaded lounge chairs and headed straight to the ocean without coverups this time. She dragged along a big foam float, dunked her whole body in the water then threw herself up on the lounger.

The water was shallow and fairly clear, the softly lapping waves kicked up enough sand to keep the water from being totally transparent. Still she could sometimes see colorful groups of fish swimming by and little creatures scurrying around the bottom. She was glad to keep her feet off the bottom. It was not enough to keep her out of the water though. She did not realize how much she needed the break. A break from the craziness of the city, her job, both of which she loved, but with the holidays coming up she could go back feeling rested and refreshed. And she did have something else to possibly look forward to. If things went well with Sean this evening she was hoping to keep things going back at home. She stopped her thought for a moment, she had not actually asked if he was from New York, she had just assumed based on his relationship with James. It was not possible that it was not his home base though. She threw some water across her body, she was getting ahead of herself again. She was looking forward to dinner and the rest of the night and that is where she should leave things for the moment.

A few hours later she wandered over to the pool bar to grab some lunch and a drink. She grabbed a table under a fan and sat watching the television behind the bar. Having borrowed paper and a pen she started making a list of things she needed to do to create a new charity. She would have to contact a hospital, her brother's girlfriend would work for that. She would have to contact the city and create a non profit organization, get a tax exempt number, find donors. It would take some work and time and with the holidays coming it may not happen until the new year. She was still hoping James wanted to be involved.

Speaking of James, there he was with Sean and they were heading her way. She supposed she would have to get used to seeing both of them together. Maybe back home it would be a more rare occurrence. She had to let her feelings for James go and hopefully this evening would help her do that. Then it would be easier for her to be around both of them at the same time.

She took a long swig of her coconut rum drink when the two men sat down, one on each side of her. They both looked at ease, even very pleased with themselves. Sean placed a large envelope in front of her which he motioned for her to open. She pulled out a small stack of glossy 8 by 10's. The first one was Kelsey in a serious glamour pose, looking well beyond her years. The next was more youthful with bright eyes and a smile that invited everyone to have fun on the beach with her. "She looks great," Allie said looking at Sean and James for agreement.

James jumped in first, "she could not have done it without you."

Sean nodded in agreement, "keep looking."

Allie flipped though a few more and came to a shot of her and Kelsey together. They were both laughing, kicking up the water at each other. She smiled as she flipped through a few more; the two of them walking hand in hand, spinning in circles and an angled shot of her sitting on the rock watching as Kelsey moved though her poses. She thought they were nice photos and was wondering if they had extra copies that she might be able to keep. She smiled as she handed the stack back, "they are nice," she said a little unsure as to how she was supposed to react.

Sean took them and spread the ones of her and Kelsey on the table, "the company wants one with you and Kelsey together."

"What?" Allie asked in shock, "how did they know you even took those, heck I did not know you did that."

Sean shrugged, "I shoot when I see something good and I forgot when they started uploading them."

Allie gave a slight look of disbelief then turned to James when he added, "they know what they want and they love these. You will get paid, you just need to sign a release."

Getting paid for a photo was the last thing Allie expected, "I don't know what to say. I am not a model. I did not even have much makeup and my hair was in a messy ponytail."

Sean put on his best smile, "some are just naturally beautiful." He ran his hand down her cheek making her blush.

"You don't have to be a model," James interjected slightly gruff.

Allie looked back at Sean still feeling slightly heated but wanting to somewhat change the subject. "Well I don't know about getting paid."

"That is what I am here for," James said quickly. "I will make sure you get a fair amount."

"Oh I am not worried about that," she paused for a moment when a sudden idea came to mind. "Hey, if we start this foundation do you think they will donate some makeup?"

James sighed, maybe a little too heavily but how could he not try. "I will see what I can do."

Allie was back in her room getting ready. She had agreed to meet Sean for dinner. It was her last night and expected it to be a good one. She chose a short dress with a scoop back and threw her hair into a loose ponytail and finished it off with strap heels. She thought she could not have planned a more perfect trip. It was a turning point for her since her move to the city. Ironically she had to go the the Caribbean to find a new relationship and start a charity. All the things she had planned to do back at home somehow started in the tropics. She caught one last look at herself in the mirror and was pleased. Maybe she could hold her own amongst all the models she thought to herself.

She walked over to the balcony doors catching the start of the sunset. She was waiting on James who wanted to walk her over to meet everyone for dinner. He was once again dining with Kelsey and her mother. She felt only a little bad that she would not be joining them. She did want to spend more time with Kelsey although she had a feeling she would see a lot more of her in the future. She was more interested in getting to know Sean better and see if there could be a future with him.

Allie was getting impatient as she truly was looking forward to her dinner date, she was getting ready to bang on the bathroom door just as James opened it and stepped out. They had a rather awkward moment of silence as they took each other in. As always James looked handsome in a pair of slightly fitted trousers, a glimmering silk shirt paired with beach sandals; only he could make his choice of clothes look good. Even if he wore sweats Allie thought she still would not be able go without an inner reaction that clouded her brain. Only when she noticed his eyes gazing over her did she look away. He made his choice she reminded herself. She brightened her eyes and smiled, "ready to go?"

With pursed lips he nodded and headed to the door.

A small crowd was gathering in the lobby. Most of the crew and models were meeting up for a celebration dinner. It seemed that it had been a successful trip for everyone all around. Kelsey was still beaming with excitement. She had new photos for her portfolio and new found confidence in front of the camera. She ran up to Allie and gave her a huge hug jumping up and down exclaiming her joy over the photo of her and Allie that had been chosen for an ad campaign. When Kelsey finally let go of her she saw Sean off to the side talking to one of the crew. Shabby casual seemed to be the norm for him and it suited him well and when he added a slight smile at seeing her Allie felt her excitement rise. She gave her farewells and best wishes to the few people she had met knowing that she would not likely see them the next day as her flight home was fairly early. James was the last one she needed to speak with. Not to say good bye though as they would be flying back together. She lightly touched his shoulder so he would turn to her.

She hesitated as their gaze met, she could see more life in his eyes now, but not totally free of trouble. She would still be there for him and she hoped this trip was not necessarily a turning point for him, perhaps more like a jumping off point for him to move forward. Just as she was about to do. "This has been an amazing couple of days."

He looked down without a response then she said quietly what he was anticipating, "I don't know when I will be back tonight."

James forced a smile and nodded. He watched her turn and join her date for the evening.

The mood on the flight home was subdued. Whether the passengers had gone to the tropics for business or pleasure there was no denying the beauty and how it affected people. And now they were all heading back to a cold and grey city. Soon though the holidays would bring color and an uplifting spirit to the atmosphere. For Allie it would be a busy work season. There would be parties aplenty but not for her to attend. It was important for the hotel to have a successful holiday season with as few problems as possible and it was her job to make sure that happened. She closed her eyes accepting her last hours of relaxation. She was tired, only from a lack of sleep that night. Dinner had been lovely with endless conversation about the city, travel, childhoods. Afterwards they spent some time walking on the beach watching the stars. There had been a shooting star, Sean told her to make a wish. Her wishes were already coming true but she pretended for him and to herself as she refused to make a specific one. The rest of the night though she did not have to pretend. she opened all of her senses to Sean, feeling all of his touches and soft kisses. Her decision to not date for so long exploded in full force as she enjoyed every moment of his attention. Her fingers tingled at the memory giving her a buzz which was a much better feeling then the alcohol induced one she had earlier in the trip. Sean had been better company, emotionally and physically then she expected and was looking forward to seeing him again.

James was also feeling the effects of lack of sleep. He had spent the night by himself though. He did admit that it had been a successful weekend. He had a new client that was starting a successful career. He finally let out his past and was working on letting it go. The hard part was that he would have to focus on something else. He knew Allie meant well wanting him to get involved with this cause, give him something to focus on. Kids though? Exactly what he did not want to focus on. Of course she did not know that at the time. It would be too emotional, too hard and he did not want hard right now. It was hard seeing Allie with Sean at first. Now he was glad her focus would be off him and trying to fix him.

He had just grabbed a beer at the bar when he saw them strolling on the beach. He planned on heading back to the room and stopped when he saw Sean pointing at the sky. Of course a shooting star, how romantic for them he thought to himself. It seemed all of Allie's wishes were coming true. He certainly had no need to make a wish, everything was just as he wanted. There would be less pressure from work, no need to find Allie a boyfriend. He was free, free to do.... he shrugged off the blank answer and closed his eyes.

James insisted they share a cab even though they lived on opposite ends of the city. He would always be Allie's friend and he decided he would be happy for her and Sean. When they pulled up in front of her building he got out to get her suitcase out of the trunk. They walked slowly to the doors despite the cold air.

"This trip was amazing; you, Kelsey, Sean, the beach, the photos."

James had a sincere smile this time, "are you going to see him again?"

"Next week, when he gets back from Rome."

"Of course, always in demand he is."

Allie smiled and looked into James' eyes, searching. He seemed happier, still she needed to ask one last time, "unless....."

His eyes shifted ever so slightly, he had to cut her off, "unless," he started to finish for her, "unless his plane gets delayed or has to run off somewhere else, then you will have to wait a few days longer. He will get back though."

"Oh yes, definitely," she agreed. She was not disappointed, she felt settled and ready to move on. "Lunch then," she said with finality.

"Absolutely," he said heading back to the cab.

She watched as he got back in the cab and was ready to turn away when he popped back up. "Shooting Star Wishes," he called out. "That is what you should name your foundation. They can make a wish with every makeover."

Allie was stunned, the buzz in her nerves coming back. He had actually been thinking about it and came up with the perfect name. "I love it," she called back to him. She watched him close the door to the cab. She had planned on closing the door on the little piece of her heart that was his. Now it was left open a crack.

Chapter 7

Life breezed by just as the cool air breezed in. Halloween and Thanksgiving both came and went then snow dusted the ground. Allie stayed busy focusing on her job. Halloween saw the hotel ballroom turned into a haunted disco for a corporate event. Special brunch and dinner menus were offered for Thanksgiving. Alex drove up from school to spend the holiday with Katie. Allie was able to see her brother for a few hours before work. She savored the turkey leftovers from Katie's mother's home cooked meals. She was thankful she walked everyday after eating turkey, stuffing, potatoes and corn bread for several days.

Next up was Christmas and another run of holiday parties. Every weekend was booked solid at the hotel. Allie needed to coordinate with various party planners, flower shops, decorators and caterers. She kept the staff at their best, or tried to. She promoted Jenny to assistant banquet director. It was too much to handle both the hotel management and the parties. Still she felt things were under control and going well enough except it was leaving her little time outside of work. Even with her longer work days she often found herself checking on things from home.

She still met up with James on occasion for lunch. They were trying to get things moving with the Shooting Star Wishes foundation. He was working on getting makeup donations. She was setting up the non profit status. It was moving more slowly then she wanted but she hoped to get it started right after the new year. And amongst all that she was making sure she found the time to see Sean. Her relationship with him continued where her and James left off. He was now the one who took her to dinner, shows and galleries. And that was in between her work and his traveling. It was everything she wanted she kept reminding herself.

Allie had been wanting to get together with James to make more plans for the charity and really just hang out with her friend. An early December snow had started falling on one of her days off. James had called to see if she wanted to meet for lunch. Truth was she just wanted to stay at home wrapped in blankets staring at the television watching meaningless shows. It was not something she did often, sometimes she just needed a pointless day. She refused to check her email and let any work call go to voice mail. Except when James called, she had no problem answering for him. Despite wanting to see him she had no desire to set foot outside in the cold. For a very brief moment she almost declined his offer to come to her place. And after she did agree and they hung up she almost wondered if it was the best idea. She remembered their kiss and the silent question asking if she should stay with Sean. And she was with Sean now so things were different. It was just going to be two friends hanging out.

After hours of mindless entertainment Allie made an effort to cook some food. She put together a basic meatloaf with roasted potatoes and set the timer on the oven. She curled back up on the couch and only realized she dozed off when the oven timer started chiming. After a big stretch and yawn, she fingered combed her hair. In her small place it did not take long for Allie to unlock the door, set the table and get dinner laid out.

As if on cue there was a knock on the door and she let James in. Giving him a sleepy smile she said, "hey thanks for coming over. I was not quite in the mood for going out today."

James let out a slight laugh, "sure no problem. Maybe someday you won't live so far away," he stepped into Allie's apartment. He had never actually made it inside her place. Had he done that on his previous visits he may have gone further than he wanted. Now, knowing she was with Sean he was comfortable hanging out with her. Even if she was still cute in her loungewear she was now taken. He looked around, her place was small and bare but livable. There were a few pictures of her and her brother and a few others he did not recognize, likely friends from before moving to the city. What little decor there was included bold colors of blues and chocolates. He decided to be polite, "nice place."

Allie smirked, "liar. It is too far from everything and it is too small. Still I am living here rent free for a year so I am grateful. I have no interest in spending my money on decorating it. I am saving all my pennies to move some day. Come sit and eat," she gestured to the table.

"Smells delicious," he said sitting down. "Rent free?" asking with a raised eyebrow. "Maybe you should stay."

"Long story," she started cutting the meatloaf into slices. "It belongs to my brother's girlfriend's friend. She is married now, anyway she decided she would let someone use it for a year at a time to help them get started or back on their feet or whatever is needed. I am the lucky first one. And since I am not exactly helpless I definitely will not be staying past a year."

James nodded while chewing. "You are lucky. I can hook you up with a real estate agent when the time comes.

"Thanks, how is work going?"

"Good," he said shrugging his shoulders. "Finished fashion week, spring catalogs are being put together. Kelsey has had a few more photo shoots and is doing well. I picked up a new client last week. Usual stuff. How about you?"

"I feel like an unwanted party guest most of the time. I have to make sure events are going as planned, I go in and check on things. I have to make sure I don't overstay, I have to turn down polite offers of food or party time. I know it's my job and I enjoy it most of the time. It just leaves me with no time to actually attend any myself. Christmas and New Years are both on weekends this year. So work for me. Not that I have anywhere to go. Anyway it is all good. I am just babbling."

"It is fine. I have not gone to many holiday parties myself this year. Just two for work."

"That is two more than me."

"You are not missing much, they are pretty much the same anyway. Too much drinking, doing and saying thinks you wished you had not."

"Oh yeah?" she asked with a raised eyebrow, "anything you want to share?"

"No," he said curtly.

"Fine, then I will just ask Sean," she laughed at the daggers he shot back at her. "Don't worry I won't judge."

It only took a second for James to relax. "He won't tell, especially if he does not want me tell you anything about him." He watched her look a little defeated. She did not need to know about his days of foolish flirtation, drunkenness and crazy dares. Not that he thought she would be bothered by it. Those days were mostly over for him. He was pretty sure it was the same for Sean as well. "How is Sean anyway?" he asked

"He is good. We don't see each other as often as we would like. Both of our jobs are always getting in the way. So far so good though," she said a little flat. She did enjoy her time with him, she was still figuring out where he would fit into her life especially with his perpetual travel and busy schedule. She had no idea how long she would have to work weekends. She kept reminding herself to not look too far into the future, enjoy her time with him. She was not sure if they were a good fit long term, some of the puzzle pieces did not fit quite right, and she had to keep reminding herself to not even think that far ahead. Again, fun right now, not perfection. And her time with Sean was fun. Time to move on to the real reason James was over.

Allie stood up to clear the table. Her mind was still drifting and had no idea in which order events took place. She only knew that she stumbled, the left overs barely made it to the counter and another mug was shattered on the floor.

James jumped up to assess the situation. "Are you okay?"

Too tired to be embarrassed Allie just flopped in a heap on the floor laughing hysterically. "Totally fine. I think my coffee mugs are in danger here though." From a little ghost girl apparently. Allie was not sure if she should tell James, she did not know if he would think she was crazy.

She was not so sure she was crazy even in believing she had a ghost. “Molly told me her little sister sometimes can do some strange things.”

“Little sister?” James did not recall seeing a little girl around.

“A ghost, her name is Julie,” Allie said cautiously.

“Hello Julie,” James said as he started picking up the broken ceramic pieces. He was not necessarily a true believer but he did not want Allie to think he thought she was crazy. When they were done he grabbed Allie’s hand and helped her up. He did not think he pulled that hard but somehow she ended up falling into his chest. As was natural he wrapped his arm around her to keep her from stumbling again. A battle between his brain, heart and body quickly erupted. It took massive will power to let her go. Somehow he managed to step back without revealing his desire to hang on.

They both cleared their emotions as quickly as the broken mug was swept away. Allie made a quick decision to go ahead and sit on the couch. She sat on one end, legs crossed and angled herself towards the middle. She watched as James came over and went back to business.

“We need more people involved with the charity. I can think of a few people. How about you?”

“My secretary, Cheryl, for sure, she is very cheerful and loves kids. I also have a friend, Gregg, he is a makeup artist. The kids will love him.”

She was beyond happy that he decided to help her. While he did not seem to be jumping for joy, he was putting thought into the ideas. She added Katie as a link to finding the right kids to work with. She recalled Molly’s mother in law enjoying event planning. And of course she would have to include Jenny from work, she could help with the costume donations and decorations.

They debated over where to hold the event. Allie assumed they would have it in the hospital. James rejected the idea. "Too depressing," he said. "That is where the kids have to get all the treatments. Besides they probably will not let us in the rooms with the sick kids."

"That is where they need the most cheering up though," Allie argued back.

"I agree, I just do not think they will let us waltz in for a makeover if they are that sick. Their bodies can not fight off regular germs like we can."

Allie pondered that for a moment and decided he was probably right. "Okay, we can set up something at the hotel. I am sure they will agree to donating the space." They continued making lists of who to ask for makeup and costume donations. They planned on having a small event to start with. If that went well they would consider a fund raiser then a larger event. They planned on another meeting just after the new year to include more people.

After feeling like they had a productive discussion they decided to watch some television. They laughed and poked fun at the reality shows. They wondered if they could race around the world. Allie said she could not survive freaky food contests and James had no interest in having to sleep outside, or getting dirty, or having limited funds.

They talked about the upcoming holiday and their plans. James would spend the day with his family. New Year's Eve would be spur of the moment. Of course Allie would have to work but she planned on spending some time with her brother.

"How come you don't have a tree or any decorations"? James asked.

Allie shrugged her shoulders. "I don't know, too much work I guess and no one here to see it."

"I am here," he answered.

Allie looked at him a little oddly but their conversation was interrupted by a knock at the door. Allie was not expecting anyone. She asked James to see who it was, she focused back on the show thinking it was likely someone she did not know. She jumped up quickly when she realized she recognized the voice. And it was not a happy voice.

James opened the door a touch and more fully when he saw Sean. "What are you doing here?" he asked James walking past him looking for his girlfriend.

Whether he meant to or not, Sean slammed the door shut with a loud bang. Allie felt a cool breeze then jumped, again when the sound of ceramic crashing and shattering reach her ears. She hoped she would get over the jitters of having her boyfriend and best friend in the same space at once. And she hoped the mug breaking would slow down, at this rate she would run out in a few days.

"Relax man, we were just talking about the charity." He knew it was his time to go. He grabbed his jacket off the back of the chair, "good night Allie, talk soon." He felt bad leaving her with another broken mess, given the circumstances he decided to leave anyway.

Allie waved him off. Turning back to the kitchen she decided she would have to make a conscious effort to put the mugs in the sink. They might be safer there. After picking up the few broken pieces, luckily it did not shatter to bits, she went to give Sean a kiss of greeting but he backed away. "Hey, everything okay?"

"I don't like him hanging out here," he answered still looking around for any evidence of unsuitable activity going on.

"We were really just talking." And she had no idea Sean would stop over, it was not something he normally did. She would not say it though, it would make it sound like she was hiding something from him. She also gave him no reason not to trust her other than the fact he knew she had been interested in James at one time. He would have to trust her and she would not beg for that trust.

"Could you have your meeting somewhere else, more public maybe."

"I did not feel like going out today. You can believe me or not." She looked at his tight face and took his hands, "I am glad you came."

Sean sighed and dropped his head. "I am sorry, we just don't see enough of each other."

"I know, I do not know how to fix that. I work, you work and travel."

"Come to Rome with me next week. Don't worry about the money."

She wished she could jet off whenever she felt like it. And she knew he would cover the expenses. It was not the point though. She wanted to be successful and independent, and her career was important to her. "You know I can't do that right now. I promise after the holidays I will try to make that happen." She reached up and pressed her lips to his. She felt him soften and open himself up to her. She let her tingling nerves take over and walked him over to her bed as she lifted his shirt over his head. He easily succumbed to her advances, he just as swiftly dispensed of her clothing and wrapped himself around her.

The next morning Allie made them both breakfast. It was earlier than she was used to but he had to be off to work. She did not mind though. After making love they talked about making more time for each other and she felt like one of the imperfect puzzle pieces suddenly slid into place.

A week and a half later was Christmas week. Allie had tried to convince her mother to come and visit. Her brother was in town again. He was staying with his girlfriend Katie. She had recently moved into her own apartment. It was too much to have Alex visit at her parents house. They loved him but between her parents and two of her brothers still living there she needed her own private space.

Ultimately their mother had declined the invite. The owner of the estate she lived and worked on was hosting the holidays at the vacation home. She claimed she was needed there. Allie knew her mother hated the city and was comfortable with the fact her mother had a close knit group of friends that would take care of her during the holidays.

Allie was invited to Katie's family house Christmas Eve morning. She had reserved Christmas morning and the rest of the week for Sean. He still wanted her to go away with him, she needed to be on stand by for work. He finally agreed to be a city Christmas guide. They went to see the towering Christmas tree in Rockefeller Center. They went at night to see it all lit up in its majestic glory with the angels lining the walkway before it. They went to the crafters market in Columbus Circle at the entrance to Central Park.

The also went to Bryant park where there was another craft fair and an ice rink. There was also a Christmas tree, though not as tall as its more famous counterpart it was decorated with actual ornaments. Allie thought it had more character that way.

She coerced Sean into ice skating at Central Park. She loved being in the park surrounded by the tall buildings. She had no problem with skating, having skated on the frozen ponds as a kid. Sean could get around without falling as long as no one was in his way. A few times she had to grab him and skirt him around a few crash landings that happened in their path.

Two nights before Christmas Allie was called into work on her normal day off. They were finishing dinner at his apartment and had planned on a movie marathon with a bottle of wine. Sean was not happy about her leaving. Allie was annoyed that he felt she should blow off her job. She promised to return and when she did just a few hours later she showed him how much she missed him.

Allie was honored that a family she hardly knew would host a holiday breakfast essentially just for her. It was partly for her brother as well but he would be with them the next morning. Rose and Katie had insisted she spend some time with their family. Allie picked Christmas Eve as she did not feel comfortable intruding on the actual holiday. She carried small trinkets for Alex, Katie and her parents. She could smell the cinnamon buns, home made she assumed when she stood outside the apartment door. She was greeted by Katie who introduced her to the rest of the family. Typical that they were hanging around the kitchen as the food was being prepared. Hands trying to steal the food were being swatted away.

Alex was helping set the table. He seemed so at ease amongst the boisterous group. Their family gatherings were quiet with just the four of them, their parents often being too tired from working hard to entertain their own guests. She observed how Alex and Katie interacted. They had the appearance of being an odd couple but somehow seemed to function as one unit.

It made her think of her relationship with Sean. After spending more time with him they were growing closer. She had been too busy to get together with James so that was no longer an issue. They were enjoying each others company and the physical part was very nice as well. She could not point out what was different with her relationship from what she saw with her brother.

Her thoughts were interrupted with a tap on the shoulder, "young love is a beautiful thing," Rose said to her.

"Yes, I am happy for him," Allie turned to face Katie's mother. "He broke a lot of hearts you know. Katie must be very special."

"She is," her proud mother affirmed. "So he had a lot of girlfriends?"

"Oh no," she did not mean to give a wrong impression of her brother. "A lot of girls wanted to date him. Always the cool surfer boy. What they did not know was how incredibly smart his is, he hid it well. Really he just wanted to hang out with his friends. Or maybe we both just wanted to make sure we made it out."

"Rough childhood?"

"No, just wanted more than small community life." She did not add they did not want to be stuck catering to the wealthy all their lives like their parents did. Even though they both were in fields where they had wealthy clients it was not quite the same as day to day serving. She did not know how much Alex told them about their lives and did not want to divulge more than he wanted.

Rose took the hint and changed the subject, "Alex tells me you are seeing someone. How is that going?"

"Good," Allie said with a slight smile.

"Ah, not the love of your life though," Rose said with a wise woman's insight.

"Well I really like him, I don't know about love." She was glad the word had not yet come up. She was not sure how she would react if Sean told her he loved her. They were having fun, no need to be serious.

"Your heart will tell you when you find it." It was such a short response yet it hit Allie like a ton of bricks. She unwillingly flashed to the day she met James. Her heart did that not her brain. She shook it off, she did not need to have what her brother did. She did not need to settle down, besides there was surely more than one person she could love out there.

She pushed those thoughts out of her mind. She focused on enjoying her morning. The family treated her as if she was a part of it and not someone she just met. Allie devoured the delicious breakfast. The conversation flowed easily and she regretted she would have to leave but she was sure she would be seeing more of them. After passing out her gifts and thanking the family for their hospitality she left to head to work with the new umbrella her brother had promised.

Her work day went relatively smoothly. The hotel guests were in a festive mood, some a little silly drunk but not troublesome. Allie gave her employees a variety of goodies including handmade candy, mints and small bottles of liquor filled chocolates. Some of them she knew had volunteered to work the holidays as they had no where else to go, some did not celebrate Christian holidays and others she knew were missing out on family functions. She appreciated every single one of them being there and wanted to express her thanks for their loyalty and hard work.

The one thing she was looking forward to was Sean meeting her at work to ride the train back to her place. Rose had sent her home with pastries and she planned on having an intimate morning with her boyfriend. Mimosas and cinnamon rolls and Sean without his clothes cheered her up and got her through the rest of the day.

He arrived just as her shift ended, candy cane hot chocolate in hand. It was a cold evening and she appreciated the warm drink for the walk to the train. More than that she appreciated the warmth of walking with Sean. It would have been a lonely ride home despite the crowds even at the late hour. She snuggled into him and let her body relax.

They walked quickly to her apartment as she knew how they would warm each other up again. She let them in and was stopped in her tracks. She was surrounded by white twinkling lights. They were hung around her windows, across her kitchen and crisscrossed her ceiling. There was a four foot tree next to her television. A little Charlie Brown style since it was so close to Christmas, it was covered in lights and stars. Stars of all sizes and colors, nothing else.

She looked at Sean expecting him to confess. It was not her, somehow it did not seem very important to her to decorate.

Instead his response was, "hey this looks great. I was not going to say anything but," he said drawn out, "I am glad you decorated."

Allie's heart stammered, if it was not him then who? She held her composure and smiled. She knew who and could not tell Sean. "I am glad you like it," she said, "I will be right out," she said heading to the bathroom. She did drink a hot chocolate after all.

She pulled out her phone and texted James, 'did you do this?' she thought to silence her phone.

Thankfully he responded quickly, 'Merry Christmas,' was the only reply.

'It's beautiful, I don't understand,' she added with some hesitation. She was almost afraid of what he would say.

She got a smiley face back along with, 'don't read too much into it. It is my present to you and Sean, you can't have Christmas morning without a tree. How is Santa supposed to come?'

She was not sure if she believed him, 'okay, thanks and Merry Christmas to you too.'

She turned off her phone and sat for a moment. Don't read into it. Really, was she supposed to believe that? Maybe a girlfriend would do that, even her brother but a guy friend though? Or just a really good friend, and that was what James was. Nothing else to read into. She went out to the man she intended to spend the special day with. They indeed warmed each other up and nestled into each other for the rest of the night.

The morning started the same way the night had. Allied opened up her senses to Sean and let her body be pleasured in ways long dreamt of. She returned the favor exploring every square inch of Sean. They found a rhythm that brought them to emotional and physical peaks together.

Eventually Allie dragged herself out of bed. She poured the mimosas and put the pastries on a plate and returned to bed. She bit into the sweet cinnamon roll letting the sugar sit on her lips. Sean leaned in and helped her clear her sweet lips with his own. She pushed him away knowing she purposely teased him. It was Christmas morning after all and that meant presents. They had agreed to minimal gifts being the relationship was so new. Allie had racked her brain for a long time trying to figure out what to get Sean: world traveller.

She reached under her bed and handed over three wrapped gifts. The first was a new pair of leather sandals. She had noticed him wearing them on the beach and they looked a little worn and later on peaked at his size. The second smaller package was a watch that could show multiple time zones. "So you always know what time it is where we both are," Allie said, although stating the obvious.

"I love it," Sean responded sincerely.

Allie watched as he slowly tore through the last box and smiled as he picked up a small white flowered printed bikini. With his head tilted and squinted eyes he said, "I am not sure this is going to fit."

She grabbed it out of is hands, "this is what I am going to wear when we go on our next trip together. Somewhere warm I hope, unless there is an indoor spa then I guess it is okay."

"I suspect it will not be staying on you very long either way," he said with a sultry look. He leaned in and stole a quick kiss, "so then, next trip you are coming with me?" he asked with a note of caution.

"Absolutely," she said, "you name the time and place and I will be there." Allie was ready to show she was committed to improving their relationship with the holidays coming to a quick end.

"Perfect," Sean said as he got up and grabbed a few small boxes for Allie. The first one contained a bottle of sunscreen and a variety of massage oils. "Ooh I like the look of this," she said. The second contained a brightly colored sarong that happened to go well with the bikini she had given to Sean, well herself really. She smiled and wrapped it around herself. The last box was small and flat, she had no idea what would fit in that. She slid the ribbon off and slowly raised the top. Pushing aside the tissue paper she saw a picture of a beach front cottage. Noticing there was more underneath, she found two tickets to St. Kitts. She could feel the sun warming her already. Only when she saw the dates did she feel the excitement ooze out of her. She did promise him though, she smiled, "this looks heavenly." That was the truth.

"Are you sure?" Sean asked noting the slight concern she was trying to hide. "I hope you can take the time off, it is just two days with your days off."

The trip was Saturday to Wednesday, she did not think that was the problem. "It is fine." She looked at the tickets again, "late afternoon flights?"

"Last minute, that was all I could get. Besides we can do some preflight lounging," he said with a suggestive look.

Less time to see the island she thought to herself, that was fine though. She did have to express her other concern, "the days off should not be an issue, it's just that we are pushing forward to setting up a date to do our first makeover with the kids and I think it will be sometime in January."

Then it was his turn to look concerned. Allie picked up the bikini, "don't worry I will make it work," she said. This was for them and she needed to make time for that as well.

"Okay," he said softly, "sometimes I feel like that is more important than our relationship."

Allie responded quickly, "I promise I will make it work." One way or another she thought to herself. She could not deny his concerns though, they were both important to her. To what degree for each she was not sure.

Chapter 8

The group met in a small conference room at the hotel. Private room in a public space, Allie could say it was to appease Sean, in reality she wanted to keep it all professional. Luckily they did not have to pay for the space. She glanced around the table. In attendance was James and his secretary Cheryl, Allie and her assistant Jenny. Molly's mother in law Susan was also there. Susan was ecstatic to be considered, having hosted many events in her life she came prepared with charts and spreadsheets. Due to work, Katie was unable to attend. She had already provided Allie with the kids support group. She had contacted them and a list of appropriate kids was being gathered for her. Most of the kids would be cancer survivors or those undergoing outpatient treatment.

James already had a supply of donated beauty products, they would use and give individual makeup kits to each child. The boys would have their choices of different face paintings, as would the girls if they chose not to do a makeover. The older girls could also get a lesson in makeup application. They were not sure about the hair situation, some kids would not have hair others might have wigs. "We want to take the focus off the hair loss and accentuate the natural beauty," James commented.

"Then we will add some bling," Susan said. "Earrings, necklaces, maybe some woven flower wreaths. We can get some ribbon and silk flowers for them."

"Don't forget we have a very limited budget right now. I can purchase some supplies, we still need to get as many donations as possible." Despite the generous check she received for the photo of her and Kelsey she needed to spread out the funds. Allie almost did not want to mention it as she thought the wreaths would be beautiful, "I am just not sure about the time to make them."

"No problem," Susan said with a smile. "I have plenty of friends with plenty of free time. And don't worry about the cost. We will just need official donation letters, for tax breaks," she added.

"No problem then," Allie said reminding herself to keep track of sponsors. They also decided on some capes and scarves, more for the boys as pirates and superheroes along with eye patches, fairy wands and swords.

Cheryl knew of a printer for invites and banners. James had confirmed with his hair and makeup stylist; Gregg. He was excited to help out. The hotel had agreed to donate the space.

That left one detail, "how does the schedule look for the space?" Allie asked her assistant. They had agreed that a Saturday would be the best day, most parents would be off and they would not have to compete with Sunday religion services.

Jenny had the computer on scanning the schedule. Allie looked over, she expected more choices. Since she promoted

Jenny she did not keep as much track as the bookings as previous. "Do we not have anything open?" she asked with a hint of curiosity.

"We booked a bunch of end of year banquets. Wait, here we go, Saturday January 16, we have a half day opening with enough time to reset for the evening banquet."

Allie grimaced as each person checked their schedules and agreed that the day would work. "Great then, it's set. Why don't we meet in two weeks? Same place and time?"

The meeting broke and they said their farewells. James lingered behind, although Allie wished he did not. She gathered up her papers and put them in her bag. She was preoccupied with the logistics of the upcoming event, she not did hear James the first time.

"Are you hungry?" James said little more loudly.

"What? Oh no, I mean I am meeting Sean for dinner." She did not know why she felt suddenly flustered. James had looked happy for a change, contributing ideas and volunteers. He surprised her and she did not know how to handle his new found enthusiasm. Be happy for him, it was what she wanted for him. "You had a lot of great ideas today," she said as they walked out of the room.

James noticed Allie seemed antsy, maybe she was running late. He did not think so, she had not been able to look straight at him since the meeting broke up. "Are you all right, the meeting went well."

"Yeah, it was great, I can't wait."

"Allie," James grabbed her arm to stop the brisk walk she picked up. "What is going on?" he asked more insistently

She stopped and closed her eyes, she should leave him out of it. Keep them separate, he would not likely let her go though. She sighed, "I am leaving for St. Kitts with Sean that day. I know I can squeeze in both, he just won't be happy about it."

"He knows this is important to you right? And if you can do both there should not be an issue."

In theory she thought to herself, with Sean she did not think so. She was not going to tell James though. "You are right," Allie said with the best look of confidence she could muster. "Thanks for everything." She gave him a quick hug and continued toward the exit.

James opened the door for her and let her go. There was something she was not saying. He would not pry, maybe watch from a distance, but not pry.

"Really? There is no other day?" Sean asked. He sat back in his chair arms crossed. They had met at an Italian restaurant for dinner. White tablecloths, candlelight and fresh flowers could not soften Sean's irritation. "Let me guess," he continued, "no other days, nothing you can do."

Allie sipped on her wine while letting Sean go on. She listened to everything she already knew, the flights were in the afternoon but he wanted to do something together beforehand. She promised she would go but she was putting the foundation before him and they did not spend enough time together. Some of what he said she knew was true but the rest she was not going to let him get away with. "We have been spending more time together."

"I know," he said slightly calmer. "I just wanted you all to myself for those days."

"You know the hotel is donating the space, so yes there were very few openings that would work for everyone." She pushed forward, she could have both, "I made a promise to you and I intend to keep it. Besides why don't you come and be the photographer?" She smiled her best pretty please smile. "Then you will be all mine." She watched as Sean swirled his wine glass contemplating. She was not giving up, "come on Sean you travel for work and I don't give you a hard time. Please, we can still be together. You don't have to be there the whole time. Just come for an hour to take some photos."

"Do you promise you will leave by a certain time, even if the event goes over? We will not be late for our flight."

"Absolutely, everyone else can handle closing and cleaning up."

"All right then, one hour for photos then we leave," Sean agreed although there was still a slight hint of reluctance.

"Thank you," Allie said as she leaned in and gave her man a kiss.

The last meeting before the first Shooting Star Wishes event was filled with excitement. The banners arrived, they had decided on a purple background with sparkling gold letters with a shooting star across the top. Gift bags were prepped with tissue paper; goodies would be added later for each individual. The wreaths were beautiful with tiny flowers and trailing ribbons. They also made sword holders for any pirates or superheroes to be.

While the hotel was slightly less busy Allie and Jenny were kept occupied with the banquet bookings. The winter events were generally less involved, end of year banquets and work conferences were the majority of the functions. It was the upcoming wedding season that was taking most of her time. They were only a few dates left and with Valentine's Day coming up she expected the last dates to be snatched up. She knew there would soon be a string of event planners, florists and brides calling her. Jenny was proving to a be a great assistant though. She was able to solve problems and had a great ability to calm distressed clients. Which meant she should be able to take a vacation without being attached to her phone. And it meant should be able to eventually ask to work daytime hours. Her plan was to overlap with Jenny and then let her handle the evening. That would be better for her social life.

For now she was excited for the next day's event, she closed her office and and went to the room holding the makeover. She walked through the lobby noting the event sign for the next day had already been changed, it welcomed the Shooting Star Wishes foundation, the Allen family reunion and a local design group's end of year banquet.

Having brought some of the decorations with her Allie went to work moving around some tables, setting up different spaces for makeup, hair and dress up. She set up a corner for the photographs. She made a mental note for next time to have some backdrops made. For now the best she could do was hang some white curtains.

Eventually she decided to go home. Not that she would sleep, she should but there was too much going on. Her bags were packed for the trip, everything was arranged for the makeover. She was looking forward to both, she wanted both to go well though she was not sure that could happen. She shook her head, everything would be fine. She turned off the lights and headed to the lobby. It was later than usual so she decided a cab would be the best way to get home. The traffic should be light making for a faster and less expensive ride home.

Allie in fact did not sleep. After returning to her apartment she checked things over again. She knew she packed her passport and i.d., her new bathing suit, sunscreen and everything else on her list. She just needed to check one more time. Once she left her apartment there would be no coming back to get anything. After placing her suitcase and purse by the door she figured a hot bath might relax her enough to get some sleep.

She poured some lavender gel into the tub and watched as the bubbles piled into foamy mounds. She lowered herself into the tub and let the hot water permeate her entire body. She closed her eyes and dreamt what the island would look like. She knew they were going to St. Kitts and the resort they were staying at. Pictures can only do so much. She only saw the few that Sean showed her. He made her promise not to research anything further. He wanted her to be surprised and he wanted the trip to be spontaneous. Not that she had a lot of time to do research so it had not been too much of an issue. She would have liked to know what some of the activities on the island and if they were renting a car. And what restaurants and bars were available. Okay so she could see Sean's point. She did wish she knew what Sean would want to do. He has been all over the world and other than taking photographs she did not know what types of activities he enjoys. She started to feel bad, she should have been asking these questions. It was not entirely her fault though. She was admittedly busy but doing the things she wanted to do, she could not see what was wrong with that.

Allie closed her eyes and tried to imagine the palm tress, white sand beach and warm tropical breezes. Her breathing was slowing as she allowed her body to relax. As she drifted deeper into her dreams of the island she could feel the water flowing over her, she was laying on a float, white billowy clouds were drifting across the sky although they seemed to be moving at an unusually fast pace. Maybe there would be a rain storm moving in later. She hoped not, the more the clouds obscured the sun the cooler she was feeling. Starting to feel a little uncomfortable she reached out for a different source of heat. She felt a hand grab hers which sent warm shivers up her arm. She was being pulled off her float, the water was even cooler than she remembered. It did not last long though, her whole body was tingling as hands wrapped around her. Fingertips traced small circles up and down her back. As they moved closer to her neck a warm body pressed against hers, she felt warm breath moving close to her. She started trembling from the anticipation. As warm lips brushed on hers her breathing quickened making her body shiver. The kiss got deeper and more demanding. Allie pressed back, her head was spinning, she pressed her toes into the sand to stabilize herself. As she dug deeper she felt a sharp object slicing into the side of her toe. She jumped back and pulled her foot out of the water and opened her eyes.

Suddenly startled Allie sat upright in the tub. The water was cold and the bubbles were down to few holdouts popping on the surface. She was in fact breathing hard and she noticed her toe throbbing. There was a slice on the side of her big toe with a small trickle of blood that was starting to stain the last of the fizzy water. She was frozen in place for a moment remembering her dream. It was like feeling physical flashes, the heat from the sun, the cool water, the warm body giving her shivers and then she really sat upright when she realized the lips that heated her up did not belong to Sean.

After her bath Allie turned on the tv, although there was mostly infomercials on. She made a pot of coffee and tried to ignore her dream. She had her foot up, bandaged and wrapped in ice. She did not want to deal with a throbbing toe and she was still unsure of how she had even managed to slice it. The end of the faucet was sharp and concluded that must have done it. Not that it mattered. She was so entranced by her dream she would never know what was happened in the real world. Once her toe settled she became antsy from the caffeine. She dressed and put on minimal makeup. After one last look around her apartment, she noted her passport safely zipped in her purse then she took her suitcase, locked her door and headed back to the hotel.

Allie did not expect any member of her group to be there just yet. She had stopped at the bakery and was putting out some plates when James came in. Allie did not expect him to be the first one to show up. Of course it was herself and him that were mostly in charge. Despite his initial hesitation he came up with the name and made sure the boys were not left out. Yet he did look disturbed at the moment. His usually cool and collected demeanor was replaced with shifting eyes and fidgeting fingers. She assumed it was not because he had the same dream she did. She squashed the memory back down and walked over to her friend.

"Good morning, I did not expect anyone else to be here this early," Allie said to him.

Pushing his hair back and stretching his neck James flopped himself onto one of the folding chairs. "I don't know if I can do this," he said quietly. He stood up again and shoved is hands in his pocket. "I mean, I will stay and help set up but I don't know if I can stay for the actual event."

Allie turned to study him. She could not quite read him except that he seemed determined not to stay. His gaze hardened as he became even more antsy. "Did something come up at work?"

That would be an easy out, but a poor excuse James thought to himself. "No, it is hanging out with the kids. I don't know if I can do it." It skimmed the surface of what he was feeling. He hoped to not have to go further, although he was sure Allie would not let him go so easily.

And she would not, "this is supposed to help you move on, I don't mean it to cause you more pain. Please stay, at least for a little while." When she saw he still looked anguished she grabbed his hand. "We will work together, it will be fine," she added trying to find the cause of his concern.

He pulled his hand away, "it is not what you think. I, just, I don't think I can do it," he said turning away from her.

"Well then what is it?" Allie asked with more persistence. She had to try just a little more, he was showing signs of life. She did not want her friend sliding backwards.

He was rubbing his balled hands together so hard, he wanted to run. There were other people who could take over and he could go back to his brooding on his own. He did not need this. He took a step towards the door when a hand stopped him. He turned to look expecting to see Allie right there but she was still several feet away. His body froze in confusion.

Allie saw the puzzled look on his face, "what is wrong?" she asked even more concerned.

James shook his head, he was sure he imagined it except the hair on his neck was raised and he felt chilled. He took a quick look around the room and saw no one else. Taking a deep breath, he brought himself back to reality, the reality that he wanted to leave. If she wanted to know then he would tell her, let her think he was a coward, he did not care. He crossed his arms and found his voice. "It's the diseases, the sick kids, the hair loss. I don't know how to talk to them, look at them."

"They are human beings James," Allie said softly. "I don't know what to expect either but I am gong to make sure I put on my best smile and make them feel welcome."

"That's easy for you, hospitality is your business."

"That is work and not always genuine." She sighed as she took a step toward him. She would let him go if she had to but it would be highly disappointing to her. "I know it's scary, but think of the kids. Think of their everyday lives and the way people look at them. People look and stare at them and not in the good way people gawk and drool over you, even if you were to lose your hair," she added. He started to seem more convinced so she went on. "Think of the treatments the have to go through and wonder if they are going to live or die. We can make one day special for them and treat them like any other kids, think of how that might give them a boost of confidence to go on and keep fighting or make them feel normal for just one day."

"You make me sound like an ass," he said with his head down and eyes closed.

"You are an ass," she said with a smile. "But," she said in a drawn out manner, "I still like you for the most part." She laughed as she messed up his hair.

He grabbed her arm by the wrist and said with hardened eyes, "don't mess with the hair." He then softened in an instant and took her hand into his. "Okay, I can manage for the next few hours." The softness of her hand helped him relax and he almost dared to pull her into a hug. Then he remembered. He let go of her hand. "In any case we need to make sure you get off on time with Sean." Did he see a slight look of disappointment before she smiled? "I will make sure everything gets cleaned up. I planned on that anyway of course, I mean I planned on coming back."

Allie shook her head, "you are still an ass, thanks for staying."

That is what he wanted, he needed to keep her at arms length, keep her focused on Sean so there would no room for him to be any closer.

Thirty minutes later the rest of the crew arrived. There was an excited frenzy of setting up hair and makeup stations, a dressing area and the photo shoot corner. They made seating areas in case the stations got backed up. A play area with a craft station was added thanks to Cheryl's last minute thinking. They did not have any true plans as to how to move the kids through the stations. Not everyone would want or need the same things. Part of Allie's plans for herself was to make sure everything ran smoothly and to help out where needed.

Allie looked around the room, everything was set up and everyone knew what their job was for the day. She was pleased with how things looked despite her desire for more decorations. Hopefully as the event drew more people they could add to it, make it more of a fantasy land. She knew this would be just the beginning and she hoped everyone here would continue with her, including James. He was talking to Cheryl and Susan. He seemed slightly more relaxed despite his fidgeting hands. She was glad he decided to stay. She watched him as long as she dared without being caught. Being his friend was easy, being just his friend was hard. Soon Sean would be there and they would be off to the Caribbean. She admitted to needing that time to focus on her relationship with Sean. She wished she could stay to discuss the day and what might be next. She would have to wait though, that she could do for Sean.

Ten minutes later her attention was solely on the kids. Kids and parents started streaming in along with Katie who reached out to bring the group together. Allie knew the kids attending were healthy enough to be there but she felt better with Katie there just in case any of the kids needed some medical assistance. Allie greeted everyone as they came in. There were more girls than boys as she expected. Most seemed to be between 6 and 12, some had hair, some likely had wigs, others wore scarves. Some of the kids were outgoing and gave Allie a big hug, others were hiding behind their parents. Allie gave those kids some space and would pay a quiet visit to them later on.

Once the majority of the group arrived, Allie knew there would be a few arriving later, she went to the center of the room to officially welcome everyone. Standing in front of the group she felt a nervousness yet excitement at the same time. This was her dream, that with the help of some great people, which was put together very quickly and hopefully successfully.

Allie put on her hospitality face she was so used to, the one with the big welcoming smile, "I want to thank everyone for coming to our first Shooting Star Wishes event. As you can see we have different areas set up for makeup and styling, dress up, crafts, a play area and we will soon have a photographer on hand as well as on site printing. There are drinks and light snacks as well. My name is Allie, I will be on hand to help where needed, as will James," she said pointing at him. "There is no particular order for you to visit each station and please only go to the ones you want."

Most of the kids jumped up quickly dragging their parents with them. A few buried their heads clinging to legs. It was the shy kids Allie was most concerned about. She walked over to a little girl hiding her head. She bent down to talk to her but she buried her head further in her mom's leg. She inched a little closer and said very quietly, "can you help me draw a picture?"

The little girl nodded her head and Allie took her hand and led her over to the craft table. "What is your name?"

"Sarah," she whispered as she took a sheet of paper and a crayon.

"That is a beautiful name," fitting for the pretty girl sitting next to her Allie thought. She had kind, sweet eyes and rosy cheeks that matched her pink head scarf. "So what should we draw?"

Sarah shrugged her shoulders as she stared at the paper. "How about I draw something first then you add to it and we will go back and forth until we have a whole picture?"

"Okay," she said quietly.

Allie started with a snowman, Sarah added a a tree, Allie drew in a house. They went back and forth until there was a dog and cat and stick figures having a snowball fight. When it was finished they both signed their name. Allie pushed it over to Sarah.

"I want you to keep it," she said quietly.

Allie was so touched she almost cried, "thank you so much," she said holding it up to her chest.

Then she saw Sarah smile and she knew the whole event was worth it. She was asking her mom if she could get some makeup and a princess dress. Allie watched her go and noticed the scene before her. She had gotten so involved with the drawing she forget to make sure everyone else was taken care of. The general atmosphere was of fun and excitement. She scanned the room in search of James. She felt like he needed a bit of attention and guidance as well. She found him wandering around seemingly making sure everyone was doing well. Allie was hoping he would be a little more personable with the kids though.

She noticed the play area was too quiet at the moment, she went over and grabbed a sword and found James. "I challenge you sir to a duel," she said with an air of authority raising the foam sword high into the air. She then looked around the room, "are there any brave souls willing to help me take on this very dangerous pirate?"

A small group of boys and girls came running yelling and screaming grabbing swords. Allie smiled at James who gave her a brief evil eye. He then ran over with a roar while racing to grab his own weapon.

An epic battle of foam swords then began. As the kids were ganging up on James he fought back with just enough effort to stand his ground while letting them win. Allie took the occasional swipe when he let a vulnerable part be exposed. He stared at her with piercing eyes that made her stop in her tracks. She shot forward in an all out effort to bring him down, even if she ended up on top of him she added to herself. She knew he could have fun with kids and was glad to see himself let go of old feelings.

"Let's get him!" she yelled doubling her efforts. A whirl wind of slashes and swinging and laughter followed. It was such a blur Allie was having trouble keeping track of what was going on. Suddenly a strong arm wrapped around her chest and she was being pulled backward into a warm mass.

James had managed to get behind her and take her hostage. She pretended to be scared while she was secretly melting inside from the heat of his body against hers. She dropped her sword and put her hands up in surrender.

"Back off or your leader won't see tomorrow," James yelled out in true pirate form.

The kids dropped their swords one by one unsure of what to do. Except one little boy who seemed genuinely concerned. He inched tentatively forward, so brave Allie thought. Some day he will make a great boyfriend. She hoped he would have that someday. The thought was brief, heartbreaking, but at least she was giving him this day.

"Who dares take this woman?" a deep voice boomed out.

James and Allie turned together as he kept his grip on her. They both stiffened at the same time when they saw it was Sean picking up his own sword with an evil grin on his face. They watched as he stood next to the little boy. "My brave friend, thank you for holding him off, I will take it from here."

Allie saw the relief in the boy's eyes as he stepped aside. She herself was not particularly relieved. Two important men in her life were about to battle it out. Sure it was play fighting but she suspected there was more on the line here. Pride for sure. She hoped they remembered kids were watching.

James spun her aside and raised his sword. The two parried back and forth as they circled each other. They slashed each other equally, luckily it was only foam. A small crowd had gathered around and the kids were yelling and screaming. She did not think they were cheering for anyone in particular just the show they were putting on. Allie was relieved when the cheering had a positive effect on them. Their intensity diminished into antics, suddenly they were swinging swords under their legs, pretending to be arrogant then falling to the floor. The kids were still cheering but laughter was the main tone now.

Allied smiled at the pair, she knew what she needed to do, "come on Sean you got this!" she yelled out. She watched as he smiled in her direction and at the same moment James seemingly tripped and fell to the ground. His sword went careening to his side as went down landing on his back.

Sean took his opportunity and pointed his sword down at him. He looked at the crowd and threw his arms up in victory. The crowd went wild. James stood up and conceded the fight graciously. He gave a slight nod to Allie as he walked away. Allie turned back and greeted her date.

"My reward!" he announced to the group. He swooped in on Allie and dipped her back and planted a soft g-rated kiss on her lips. Allie relaxed into his strong grip and smiled at him.

He let her up as the girls were giggling and the boys were saying gross. Allie gave him a hug and thanked him again for coming.

"How is it going?" he asked her.

"Great so far," she said.

"I have some equipment I need to set up," he pointed at his cases by the entrance.

Allie followed her boyfriend over to the staged area for the photoshoots. She was glad to see him. She knew he was reluctant to be there. She would have to be sure to show her appreciation. Their trip came to mind. She truly was looking forward to it. She did want to travel although she was not thrilled with the timing. She knew Jenny could handle the end of year banquets but wedding season was looming. Perhaps there was never really a good time to travel yourself when you catered to tourists and banquet clients. There never seemed to be a true down time in the city. It was what she wanted she reminded herself yet she knew she had to learn to dedicate some time to her personal life. And as she was plugging in Sean's computer she remembered she would leave all work behind and trust her associates to handle things for her. Including the charity. Even though she wanted to stay and plan the next event she could survive a few more days. Especially in the Caribbean.

As if reading her mind, "ready for our trip?" Sean whispered at the back of Allie's neck.

She let his warm breath tickle her senses for a moment. In a few hours a warm tropic breeze would add to the heat. Her excitement level inched up a notch, not a huge spike but it definitely went up. She pulled herself away from him and smiled, "all set, suitcase in my office."

"Good," he said brushing his lips across hers giving her a taste of what was to come. He took her hand and stood her in front of a green screen. "Pose," he said

Allie scrunched her face, "what do you want me to do?"

"Anything," he responded.

"Can I ask one of the kids to join me?"

When he shrugged she went in search of Sarah who quickly agreed to the picture. She had made her rounds and was glowing with her soft eyeshadow, light layer of glitter, nail polish and pink flower wreath. She had picked a pink princess dress to match.

"You look beautiful," Allie told her. She was rewarded with a huge smile.

The pair went hand in hand for their photoshoot. Allie smiled at the memory with Kelsey on the beach. Except Sarah no longer seemed the shy little girl that came in the room a few hours ago. She was a ham in front of the camera. Or maybe it was Sean who encouraged her to be silly. They laughed and giggled and posed. When Sean had enough photos they stood in front of the computer reviewing the images.

"We have a variety of backgrounds." Sean looked at Sarah, "do you want a castle, a forest, a beach?" he asked as he scrolled through several more.

Allie stood up as they played with the images. It had not occurred to her they could use digital backgrounds. Another reason to be grateful for Sean's professionalism. Returning to her own professionalism Allie knew there was another group of people here that needed support. Sarah's mom was standing there looking like she was going to cry. "Are you okay?" Allie asked her softly.

"This means so much to me and to Sarah as well. This has been so hard on her. She has been so quiet, today is more of how she normally acts. You let her be a kid again, you made it okay to be a kid again." The woman hugged Allie which almost brought tears to her eyes.

"Thank you, this is what I hoped to accomplish."

Allie made another round through the room, making sure things were going smoothly. She sent Cheryl over to help Sean with the printing of the photos. She started clearing the craft table. James was helping some boys with pirate outfits. He caught her watching him. He gave her a wink and a smile and sent the boys on their way. Allie fought not to blush, she gave him a quick smile back and turned away. Sean was still involved with photographing the kids and she was grateful he missed the brief exchange.

As she continued looking around she noticed a teen girl entering the room. She was tall and thin, her skin was pale and her eyes looked sad. She stood cross armed not sure what to do. Allie went over and welcomed her.

"I have no interest in a makeover," she said.

"You do not have to," Allie put out her hand, "Allie, what is your name?"

"Haley," she said without returning the handshake.

"Nice to meet you." Allie was trying to think quickly, "if no make over then how about a manicure?"

Haley shook her head no.

"Some photos?" she ventured although not surprised by the harsh look she got in return. She looked around and then it hit her. She nodded over to James, "I could introduce you to my friend." What teenage girl would resist meeting a cute guy?

Haley studied him for a moment then said, "sure why not?"

James was starting to clean up. Overall he was happy with how the day was going. Now he felt foolish for trying to back out. Allie for sure was happy. He kept watching her interact with the kids. She was a natural, she made him smile. She always made him smile. Then he had to pretend to be defeated by Sean. That did not particularly make him smile. He knew he had to do it. Allie belonged to Sean. And he was gong to make sure it stayed that way.

He stood up from clearing the toys on the floor and almost bumped into a pouting teenage girl. "I am sorry," he said pushing his hair to the side.

"No problem," the girl said, "I'm Haley."

"Haley is not sure how she wants to spend her time here today. I thought maybe you could hang out with her," Allie smiled sweetly at James.

He gave her a brief evil eye. He knew what she was trying to do. And maybe he needed this. Not that it made him ready to jump back into life. He looked at Haley, at least she was a teenager. He could talk to them, he did that for work everyday. In any case the event would be over soon.

"So no make over today?"

"No, what is the point?" Haley said with a slight edge of anger.

"Then let's go for a walk, we can people watch in the lobby." He looped his arm through hers.

Allie followed them part of the way, "thank you," she mouthed squeezing James' arm.

"You're welcome," he mouthed back. He strolled out to the lobby. Luckily there was seating left. He chose a small couch in a quiet area and sat down. He crossed his legs and swung in Haley's direction. Sitting felt good. He had not slept well and the day had been physically and emotionally taxing. He propped his elbow on the back of the couch and rested his head in his hand.

"Long day?" Haley asked him

"Kids are full of energy."

"They are the healthy ones," she said with downcast eyes.

"Hmm," James was nodding his head. He understood, she was not one of those kids. He was not sure how else to respond though, he did not want to have a depressing conversation and he was sure his companion did not either.

"Did your parents bring you here?"

"No," was her simple response.

"Then why are you here?"

"Something to do," she said with another one of her shrugs.

James decided to switch to what he knew best. "You know you have incredible eyes. They are so light they are almost clear. And when you do smile, it is quite stunning."

The corner of her lip started to turn up then she looked at him suspiciously. "You are just saying that."

"No," he said shaking his head, "I work with models, I know what I am talking about.

"Really?" she said smiling. "Must be difficult hanging around beautiful women everyday," she said sarcastically.

"Well someone has to do it, might as well be me."

"Do you date them?" she asked

"Nah, try not to mix work with pleasure."

"What about Allie are you dating her?"

"Allie?" he straightened up. "No we are just friends," he said leaning back into the couch again. "Anyway she has a boyfriend. How about you, any boyfriends?" he asked wanting to take the conversation off him.

"Hard to have one when you are in and out of the hospital."

"That's just an excuse." James smiled softly. "There is still a bright light in those beautiful eyes of yours."

"Well the light is fading," Haley said downcast.

James picked up the girl's slender hand. "Does that scare you?"

"No, I mean I am not scared for myself I worry about my parents though."

"So no fight left? None at all?"

"When you have been fighting all your life it wears you down, mentally, physically. My body won't cooperate anymore," she answered with a shrug but she held onto James' hand.

"How much longer?" he asked with a lump in his throat that threatened to send him over the edge.

"Don't know, she has not come yet," her gaze drifted off into the distance.

"Who?" he asked curiously thinking it would be a doctor or a special counselor.

"Julie," she said tentatively.

"Tell me," he encouraged her.

She rolled her eyes and sighed. "So there is this urban myth at the hospital. A little girl named Julie died there a long time ago. They say she wanders the halls and somehow she knows when," she paused, "you know," another pause, "when one of the kids is going to uh heaven. Anyway she supposedly tells them it is all right. I don't know, get them to the other side."

"Do you believe this legend?"

"I don't know. In a way it is scary but also comforting. They say she is always right. That is why it's a little scary."

"So you have never seen her?"

Haley closed her eyes, "there was a moment, I was sure I felt a presence. Someone holding my had, I know there was no one there. I don't know who it was, if it was Julie or someone else."

James sat quietly for a moment, he wondered if he should tell Haley about Allie's little ghost. It seemed more then coincidental that they had the same name. He suspected this was not something she shared with anyone. He let the subject drop since Allie's Julie seemed to have a different agenda in the apartment or at least he hoped so. He rubbed Haley's hand more as a calming effect for himself. He really could not imagine what she was going through. And the girl's parents. He never got to meet his child, he could only imagine what she or he would have been like. Next to him was a girl that would never experience so much in life. At least she had some part of life. Not that he would say that, that would make him sound like an ass. Either way he was sure there was nothing he could say to make her feel better.

But maybe words were not what she needed. "Do you think there is something keeping you here?" He flinched, that did not come out right he thought right away. "I mean something left you want to do." He shook his head, "sorry this is not coming out right."

"No it's okay. I know there are so many things I won't do or see. Probably the hardest thing has been not getting to be a real teenager. I will never get to go to a party, I won't graduate or learn to drive." She closed her eyes, "I won't go to a prom." She suddenly pulled her hand away, "Not that I am girly or anything."

Jame's heart was hurting. He helped make women beautiful everyday but did it actually mean anything? He was sure it did in some sense, maybe not in the grand scheme of things anyway. For this one beautiful young lady, he could do something. "Haley, would you give me the honor of being my date at our winter ball?" The group had not fully discussed the possibility of doing a full out dance but James knew he had to make it happen. And he knew he had limited time to plan it.

Haley gave James a thoughtful then hardened look. "No I will not be your date. I think that might be illegal or something."

They both had a good chuckle.

"I will go if you ask Allie to go with you. She should be your date."

"I told you she has a boyfriend, besides this is not about me."

"Are you sure?" she looked at him with a wisdom that no teenager should have. "Is all this really about me?"

"And the others too," James said a little defensively. All of this was for the kids. It was not like this event would suddenly change his mind about dating or having kids. He was still standing by his decision.

"Look, all I know is that life is too short to give up on the things that you want. We appreciate what you are doing here. And that is great if it makes you feel good. I mean it should, it's a good thing. The kids are having a great time. And yes I would love to come to your ball. Promise to save me a dance."

She stood up and pulled James up with hidden strength. "I saw the way you look at her, don't ignore what your heart is telling you."

James had no response. Maybe he would think about it another time. Likely not though. This was still about the kids and not him. He bowed slightly while softly kissing Haley's hand. He grinned when she blushed. "Don't forget you promised me a dance."

"You don't forget," she said with a wink before heading out the door.

James watched her leave, he pushed his hair back clearing his head. He would not let a teenager affect his life decisions at least not when it came to his personal life. He was happy to do this for the kids. That is where it ended. Just like business he learned to separate his business life from his personal life. It would be no different now.

He went back in the event room to fill in Allie that they now had a ball to plan. He knew she would be excited. And then he saw Sean with Allie. She actually looked happy. Happy with the events and even more so happy standing next to Sean. James knew what he needed to do at that moment. He knew she needed the next week with Sean, the planning for the next event could wait or start without her.

And he needed the next week to himself.

"You two pack up and get out of here, you have a plane to catch."

Allie turned, "are you sure, we can help clean up quick."

"We got this covered, we talked about this. Sean," he nodded to him, "thanks for coming. Now take this woman and give her the vacation she deserves."

Sean shook James' hand, "no worries, I will take care of her," he said with a wink.

James wanted to twist his hand and break his fingers one by one for putting images of him and Allie together in his mind. He gritted his teeth and accepted the handshake. Turning to Allie he said, "go, have a good time."

"Yes, we are going, just a few more minutes. I want to talk about what we should do next."

James watched as Sean gave her a look of irritation. "You promised we would leave at the end, and I need to to get my equipment back home."

After James indicated for her to get going Allie took the hint. She turned to Sean. "I am sorry, you are right, let's go."

Chapter 9

A week later Allie was sitting with her eyes closed during the plane ride home. Her hand entwined with Sean's who was focused on the in flight movie. She was comfortable and content, Sean had been fantastic indulging in her tourist whim. And in return she went with him on a deep sea fishing trip. Of course it was more sunbathing for her. She thought the jet skiing was way more fun especially when she turned too sharp and dumped them both off into the clear water. She swore she saw a huge sea turtle and was trying to avoid it. Sean claimed he saw nothing. He also claimed to have caught a huge fish which he then released. She never saw that, who was she to deny his excitement.

Her favorite part of the trip was the private dinners on the veranda of their beach front cottage. Their conversations were light and numerous with no thought of the future. That was fine with Allie, she was just enjoying herself for the moment. And she did live in the moment, in the nude, in the plunge pool, Sean savoring her body, and she exploring his.

She squeezed Sean's hand and he returned it with a soft kiss. She smiled and breathed in a relaxing breath. As much as she enjoyed the week she was a little anxious to get back. They had agreed to no computer and limited phone and no checking emails. Not that she was expecting any issues, she was more interested in the feedback from their makeover event. James rushed her out so fast she could not even ask about his conversation from the teenage girl that came in.

James, she had tried not to think of him too much during the week. She only wondered briefly how he was doing. It was a step in the right direction for her. She continued to twirl her fingers in Sean's hand. He was a good thing for her right now and who knows maybe longer.

Allie had one day off when they returned. She had to do some shift switching to get the week off. Sean had insisted on escorting her all the way back to her apartment however she insisted he go home as she was tired. She had collapsed in her bed and slept for hours. Now her Sunday was for laundry, errands and food shopping. And she knew it was everyone else's Sunday so she decided not to call anyone for an update. She would see Jenny soon enough. Or James, she would call him tomorrow. Today was too early. She could spend a quiet night by herself, she suspected a flurry of activity would be waiting for her.

Which started early the next morning. She snapped awake when she realized the knocking was not a part of her dream. Grumbling she rolled out of bed and acknowledged the rapping at her door. "What do you want," she yelled with her best it's too early in the morning voice,

"Good morning," a familiar voice responded, "I thought you might be missing a good bagel by now."

Allie was a little shocked to hear James' voice. She did smile though, she was happy to see him and she really did want to talk to him yet not seem overly anxious about it. Of course she was overthinking this whole thing. It was just her friend coming over. And all that flashed through her brain in a half a second. Her stomach grumbled and she finally breathed. Laughing at herself she said, "give me one minute."

She trotted over to her dresser while finger combing her hair, threw on a pair of jeans and a sweatshirt. She slid her feet into her ballet slippers as she flew back to the door. After unbolting the two locks she let James in. She watched him as he walked in with the white bakery box. He was his usual put together self in his long wool coat and dark scarf. While he was not quite smiling she did see a brightness to his eyes that he only let out on occasion.

Allie watched James as he turned around and wondered briefly about the size of the box from the bakery. Two bagels should not warrant such a box. Maybe there was a cheese danish she thought as she was closing the door. Only she met resistance. She turned to see Jenny, Katie and Susan standing in the hallway.

"I hope you don't mind," she heard James say. "We need to catch you up."

"We started some planning," Susan added. "We need to move quickly on some things so we need your approval." She came in with enough energy for all five people in the room. She was ready, carrying a binder with her leather gloved hands.

Allie's excitement level jumped up several notches. She let the group in and took their coats. "Are you kidding? I can't wait to hear what has been going on. You guys are lucky I bought more coffee yesterday." She pulled her desk chair over to the small kitchen table. She started the coffee and rummaged through her cabinets for enough plates, mugs and utensils. Since she generally ate by herself she had not had any excuses to buy anything matching, although she was fond of her eclectic collection. Diminishing collection, she remembered the numerous broken mugs, but she still had enough left for the group.

"Does anyone want tea instead?" she asked while putting creamer and sugar on the table. Everyone seemed good with just coffee. She set up a serving area on the small counter space so the food would not clutter the table. The group quickly grabbed bagels and pastries with the coffee and squeezed in around the table.

Allie had been patient while setting up, now she wanted, needed to know what was happening. "So give me the update," she said with an unbridled excitement that defied her grudge at getting out of bed early.

Katie started first, "the response back from the parents was amazing. They want us to do it again. Of course we need to have a different group of kids."

"Not that we would ever deny a kid from coming again, we might need to think about how many we can handle at once," Susan said in her business like manner.

"I don't think that will be too much of a problem. We can just set up an RSVP system."

"And there are different groups we can contact," Katie added. "The invitations can vary depending on what we are doing."

"Then we can send out additional invites to those who want to come back if we still have room. And a lot of that will depend on our donations and if we want to expand our volunteer base. Which brings us to our next event, James," she nodded towards him.

Allie was sitting across from him. He had been so far watching quietly not showing too much emotion either way. Typical for him she thought to herself. She took a closer look into his eyes as he swallowed his piece of bagel and sipped his coffee to wash it down. They were still brighter, maybe a shade of sorrow still there. Maybe she would ask him later. Maybe. This was where her friendship should be with him, in this group setting working on a charity. That was sensible and fair to Sean. Sensible sucks though she pursed her lips very briefly before returning her attention to James when she heard her name.

"What? I'm sorry, still a little tired from the trip," she said with a slight laugh.

"Haley, she was the girl you had me talk to."

"Yes, I remember. She never came back in for anything."

"No. I am not really sure why she came, I am not sure she even knows why. Anyway one of her wishes," he cleared his throat, "is to attend a dance." He fidgeted with his bagel, "she does not think she will live to see her prom. So, um, I told her we were hosting a winter dance." He took another swig of his coffee.

Everyone at the table was silent for a moment, obviously Haley touched James in some way and Allie could tell he was struggling with his emotions, which was really a good thing. It meant he was having feelings again. And she was not going to let him suffer. "That sounds great James, I love the idea. A lot of work, so what do we have so far?"

"Well first I want to hold a fundraiser," Susan started flipping through her notes. "I know a lot of people. We will host a ticketed dinner with a silent auction, dance floor, some kind of presentation."

"I have dates already reserved at the hotel for both events."

"Between the five of us we expect we can sell a few hundred tickets."

"Wow," Allie was impressed and excited, "that means the ballroom then."

"The dinner will be on a weeknight. The actual dance on a Friday night."

"What kind of time frame are we looking at?"

"Two and a half weeks for the dinner and four and a half weeks for the dance."

A wave of anxiety ran through Allie, "not much time."

"We have the room, I am working on the dinner menu. They donated the space and will let us do the food for cost. A few chefs and wait staff are volunteering their time."

"The tickets should be back from the printer tomorrow, I will make sure everyone gets a stack."

"And we need to get invites out for the dance as well then."

"I am working on that," Katie said. "We want it to be formal so is it okay if we go fancy on the stationary?"

"I think we can swing that," Allie said. Some of Susan's friends had already donated funds. "Send me some samples and we will choose." Allie felt like a lot of the decisions had already been made and she was generally all right with that but she wanted to make some choices as well, "anything else?"

"I know some families may have some financial issues. I was hoping we can have dresses donated at the fundraiser," Katie added.

"That sounds good. How will we distribute them?"

"We can keep them at our office, right James?" Cheryl asked looking at him. "The girls can come by to try them on."

"Sure, we will make room."

"All right then, let's meet again next week at the hotel unless we need to do so sooner. Thanks everyone."

The group split up, James lingered behind. It had been a long week for him. He kept himself busy at work and with the planning for the Shooting Star Wishes events. He was proud of himself for that. As hard as it was for him to attend the make over event he finally understood that life was not hard for him. It was hard for the kids and their families. If a few hours of his time could bring happiness to kids then he could push his own personal issues aside and deal with it.

As for the issue of Allie being in the Caribbean with another man, well that was harder to push out of his mind. He missed her bright smiles and enthusiasm. She still looked good even though they obviously woke her up. He was glad she was not mad about that but he knew her schedule. He was glad she was alone. It was a gamble going there and had assumed Sean would be back at work. He tried not to think of what they were doing and he probably should not stay to ask. But then that would not be acting like a good friend either. So here he was, he will ask bare minimum then be on his way.

He leaned on the kitchen counter while the others left indicating he wanted to stick around. When the last person left and the door was closed he sat back down at the kitchen table. He did that so Allie would not give him a welcome back hug. He did not want to know if the scent of the salt air still lingered in her hair or the coconut of sun lotion stayed in her golden skin.

Allie sat across from him all smiles, he wished he felt as relaxed as she was. Surrounded by beautiful women all day long yet this one kept him on edge, kept his heart beating, kept his brain occupied. She threw him a life line and he was circling around it, he just did not know if he was fully ready to catch it. Right now he was just bobbing with a life preserver but he could not stay there forever. Eventually he would turn into a prune. He almost made himself laugh.

"So how was your trip?" he asked leaning back crossing his arms as if they would defend him from things he did not want to know.

"It was nice," she said. "Very relaxing, St. Kitts is beautiful, lush and tropical."

"Good, glad to hear it." He leaned forward again fiddling with his coffee cup. "So um, things are good with Sean then?"

"Yeah," she said with a genuine smile. Her mind wandered back to the warmth of the tropics for a moment before focusing back on James. "How was your week? Busy it seems, I can't believe how much you guys have done."

Relieved to not get any details of the trip and to be back on common ground he said, "yes it was busy but good busy. I actually signed a new model also."

"Wow that is great, you seem to be on a good roll with that."

"And Kelsey is getting more work also, she is coming next week for a job."

"Oh we should see if they will come to the fundraiser. Maybe she can say a few words about her experience with her friend Gracie."

"It will be good publicity for both of us. I will talk to her this week."

A knock at the door interrupted their conversation. Allie looked over then stood up. She peered through the peep hole then unlocked the bolts. James watched as Sean walked though the door. He was surprised he was not at work and now he would know he was hanging out at his girlfriend's house. Innocent or not Sean probably would not like it. Which meant it was time for him to leave. He stood purposely making some noise, he did not want to see some passionate kiss. And it worked, Sean looked over Allie's shoulder. He looked annoyed, nothing James could do about it but make himself scarce.

"I'm out, I will be in touch," James said quickly as he skirted past the couple and headed out the door,

"Thanks for all the work James," she said to his back. He waved his hand back at her as headed to the elevators.

Wow that was a hasty exit Allie thought to herself. Well maybe having the two of them in her small apartment would not be a great idea anyway. She closed the door and went over to give Sean a kiss hello.

But he backed away, "what the hell was he doing here?" he asked obviously pissed off.

Allie grumbled at his reaction, "we were having a meeting, discussing some upcoming events," she said glaring at him.

"Just the two of you, here at your place. I thought we had discussed this."

She closed her eyes and sighed, yes she should explain, she just wanted a little more trust from her boyfriend. "The whole crew was here, see look at all these dishes. They brought breakfast and I did not know they were coming."

"So they left and he stayed."

"We were just catching up, what is wrong with that?"

"I don't like it," he said with a firm stance.

She walked over to him and put her hands on his chest, she could feel just a slight bit of tension come out of his muscles. "Nothing is going on between us, please just trust me."

He gave in to her touch which warmed her insides. It had only been a day and she was missing him. She pressed closer into him and ran her hand up the back of his neck. Even if they did not always agree, their bodies were certainly in tune with each other. She pressed her hips against him hoping he had the same ache she felt.

She was disappointed when he pulled back slightly. "Allie," Sean said softly, "I always feel second to James."

She took a half step back without letting go. She let her hands roam across his shoulders around his neck and cheeks. She did not want to have to try so hard to convince him, hopefully just a little reassurance would help. "I thought we were getting past this."

"You liked him first, he took you to the Caribbean first, he got here first this morning."

She almost felt bad for him except she was surely not his first girlfriend. She would have to spin it a different way. "None of that matters Sean, he took himself out of the equation. Which means you got the important first." She reached up and pulled him towards her. She pressed her lips on his demanding passion and understanding. She got the response she was anticipating. She tugged on the buttons of his jeans while pulling him to her bed. He was more than willing to accept her offer.

"This is the original soup nazi?" Allie asked James. They were on 55th Street in midtown not too far from her hotel.

James laughed but said quietly, "yeah, he does not like the word nazi though."

"Oh, okay, I will make sure to remember." They had their orders in to go cups. She did not have time to sit and eat. She missed their lunch meetings. She had never called them dates and would not start now. Just meetings with a friend and still not even a sit down meal. Food to go, on the way to work, totally innocent. She was feeling a little frustrated, she felt like she had to see James practically in secret. If it was not related to the charity then she had no other excuse good enough for Sean to see him. She was aware of jealousy and competition between men. And what would she do if the situation was reversed? She sighed knowing she would feel the same way.

Which meant she knew what she needed to tell James. They had walked the few blocks to the hotel in relative silence. As they approached the building she turned, "I told Sean I would only meet with you outside my place, which unfortunately has to include our group meetings."

James pursed his lips but he nodded in agreement. "I understand."

Mixed emotions rushed though her, she did not want him to protest, well maybe a small part of her did. She could not bare to stand to look at the distant look on his face. There was a look of hurt in his eyes. She felt the water start to sneak into her own eyes, "always friends James, right? No matter what happens."

"Always," he whispered in her ear. He put his hand on the back of her neck, holding her close as he said it. They stood like that for a few seconds taking in each other as if they were saying goodbye forever.

James stepped back first. He had a goofy grin as if the last few moments never happened. "See you Monday." He turned and blended back into the crowd.

Allie was trying her best to keep her mind on work. She was left with the task of hiring some new employees. She had just been through a round of interviews. She was not sure she was the best at judging character anymore. She tried to reread the resumes but the words just blurred. She wanted to do some internal shifting of staff but that meant more training instead of hiring for experience. Still it rewarded loyalty and hard work. She wished she could pick up the phone and ask James, he was good at judging people. He helped her once before. No, right now she needed to rely on herself.

A soft knock followed by the creak of her door brought her attention back. "Come in Jenny," she said as she pointed to the empty chair near her desk.

"What's up?" she asked in her always cheerful work manner.

"Um," focus, Allie thought to herself. "I just wanted to thank you for the work for the fundraiser and dance. As well as keeping up with things here."

"No problem. How was your trip?" she asked with raised eyebrows.

"It was good."

"Just good? What is going on?"

"Nothing, the trip was great. I just," she dropped her head into her hands, "I just feel like I broke up with my best friend."

"Did something happen with James?"

"No, not really, it's just getting too complicated, dating Sean and trying to be friends with him."

"Guys can suck sometimes."

She grinned a little, if they did not give her so much pleasure and company and giddy feelings she would not bother. She liked giddy feelings and sex too. Why did she stop for so long her body asked her. To get here, at this moment she grumbled back.

She straightened back up getting back to the business at hand. "No worries, Sean and I are happy and James is still working with us." Enough self pity she had good news for Jenny. "What do you think of Marissa from housekeeping?"

"Fine, I will change the topic. Only because I have a meeting with a bride soon," Jenny said with a slight grumble. "Marissa, she seems to work hard, does her job well."

"I was thinking of promoting her to front desk."

"Oh, I did not know we needed another person."

"With summer coming I am expanding the staff."

"Oh well then I think she is a little young but very personable, she always wants to please."

"Great then you start training her next week. I know you have meetings but after that you will start your new position and will have more time."

"What?" she asked shocked, "I have not applied for anything."

"I can't handle all the hotel logistics and the banquet rooms, I am promoting you to full time banquet director." Jenny was oddly silent. "That is if you accept. Of course there will be a raise with that and you will still have to work weekends. Maybe we can work out some weekends off depending on the schedule. We can figure something out between the two of us." Allie was rambling on since Jenny had yet to respond.

Finally she jumped up, "yes of course, thank you so much!" she ran around the desk leaning over giving Allie a big hug. "Can I tell people?" she asked anxiously.

"Just find Marissa for me then you can spread the word. Even if for some reason she does not accept you will still train your replacement."

"No problem," she said practically skipping out of the room.

Allie smiled, at least she would make two people happy today.

Allie was tired, it had been a long six day work week making up for the vacation. It was worth it of course. She just wished she did not have to leave her apartment for the meeting. It was cold, windy and it was going to start snowing later in the day. She kept her promise to Sean though and arranged for the meeting to be at a cafe. The hotel was her initial thought but she spent so much time there already.

They had eight days to finalize the plans for the fundraiser. They went over the count of tickets sold. Allie had sold some to people at work but Susan knew far more people then any of them. Katie also got a good response from her coworkers. Donations for the silent auction were coming in including a free weekend with the Blue Hotel chain as her contribution. James arranged to have decorated clothes racks sent over so the donated dresses could be hung and displayed before being sent over to his office.

Preparations for the dance were underway as well. Based on the ticket sales, they were able to buy new linens and order flowers. Catering services would be again at cost provided by the hotel. The menu would be more whimsical and kid friendly versus the elegant dishes for the fund raiser. Jenny, already stepping up to her new position, had those arrangements under control. Allie and Katie had agreed on gold invitations with purple writing, they would be going out this week

Allie looked down at her checklist. She had been double and triple checking on things during the morning hours before work. They were all probably sick of her emails by now. She trusted them of course, she just wanted everything to be perfect. She did find one box left unmarked.

"I have a photographer for the dance. I invited my old roommate up from Virginia. She does nature and wedding photography. Anyway she will be great but she can't make two trips." She spent too many hours talking to Emma Sunday morning. She really missed her friend and had been bad about keeping up with her. No hard feelings on either side as they picked up exactly where they left off. Emma was beyond happy having Ben living with her and her photography business was flourishing which was good since kayaking tours were limited in the winter.

"What about Sean?" Jenny asked.

"Fashion week is coming up," Allie said quickly. "His schedule is pretty tight right now." She stole a glance at James, he acted uninterested until she added, "he will be there he just does not know what time he can get there." James ever so slightly shook his head looking at her briefly. She gave him an equally brief glare telling him to back off whatever he was thinking. Sean was trying to support her but in his defense he was busy that week

"No worries," Susan jumped in, "I will find someone for the fundraiser. We will need publicity shots for the local papers." She smiled as she talked about a friend of her son's that would likely do it for free. It was like she sensed the brief tension between Allie and James and forced the conversation back on track.

"Kelsey is coming," James said almost out of nowhere. "She said she would speak, I managed to reschedule her photo shoot so she would not have to make two trips. She also managed to get a hold of some vintage Barbie dolls for the auction. I have a donation for a makeup lesson, photo sessions and two tickets to a runway show."

"Wow James that is fantastic. Thank you."

"Sure," he said casually. He stood up, "I have to get to work. Let me know if you need anything else."

That was the signal for the rest of the group to leave, this time Susan lingered behind. "James seemed a little off today."

More then a little she should say, she shrugged instead as if was not her business.

"Hmm," she pondered. "Did you ask Sean to do the photography?"

That was a strange change in topic Allie thought. "No, actually I just want him to be my date honestly. I know he helped out last time and he would probably do it again. It's just that he does that all day."

"No need to explain, it's good to have a date night."

"Well I am trying to show him my feelings for him are real. James is not an issue and I am working to make our relationship stronger."

"You don't have to convince me, just yourself and once you do Sean will fall in line." She stood up and while putting on her jacket added, "relationships will always take some work but you have to know what you want to get out of it."

She watched Susan leave. She had no idea what she meant by all that. She did have feelings for Sean and she was making time for him and putting his feelings first. Satisfied with her analysis she got up and left looking forward to a bubble bath back home.

And while Allie was headed home James walked back in his office. He thought he handled himself well. All business talk, nothing personal. Except she did catch his unintentional response to hearing about Sean not being the official photographer. She probably asked him and he probably turned her down. Sure it was fashion week next week but he should still make time for the person he cared about and the work they were doing. So maybe it was not Sean's work but as the boyfriend to the director of the event he should arrange to be there. Not that it was his business anyway. Her relationship, her issue to work out.

He stopped by Cheryl's desk to pick up his messages. He was hoping that she stepped away for a minute and he could just grab the slips of paper she still insisted on using. No luck though as he saw her spiked red hair peer out from behind her computer screen. She was on the phone though and he was still hoping he could grab the slips.

Again no luck, she slammed her hand down on the stack before he could grab them. She finished with her phone conversation and looked up at James. "How did the meeting go?"

"Great, can I have my messages?"

"Not yet," she said slyly.

"Come on Cheryl, I have work to do."

She contemplated making him squirm. She knew she was skating a professional line. And she knew if she had not been friends with his parents she would likely have been fired many times over. She just could not help caring for the kid. "I got a few more tickets to next Friday's runway show for the auction."

"Thanks," James said. "Can I have my messages now?" he asked again impatiently.

"You know what you need?" she asked with a grin.

"My messages," he reiterated.

"A date. For the dinner. I can help you know."

"No," he was quick to answer.

"Why not, you will just sulk over Allie and Sean. You made your choice, she made hers. Time to let go sweetheart." She picked up a folder and a stack of messages and finally handed them over, "think about it," she said with sincerity.

James went into his office. A date was not what he needed or wanted. That was his whole point all along. No more relationships, no more involvement, no more heart break. Work was his life, work and what? he asked himself. Working with Allie from a distance. Was it possible to have a broken heart without ever having dated a person. So it did not matter whether or not he dated, if he was destined to have a broken heart either way he might as well have fun. Back to being the eligible bachelor he would be. No more sulking. There were plenty of women out there. He buzzed Cheryl's phone, "okay, a date but no crazies." He hung up the phone surprised at what he did without thought. He just agreed to let his crazy receptionist find him a date. Well maybe she could in fact choose better then he could. He would find out soon enough.

Chapter 10

Allie spent most of the morning at the hotel working with Jenny. They were setting up for the dinner. Jenny truly did have everything ready to go as promised. As banquet director she had a little more freedom to work on this during business hours and Allie was fine with that. She kept up with the rest of her work. While she worked on the set up and decorations Allie sorted through the donations for the silent auction. She made flyers for each one on her computer and placed them in picture frames. She went back to the ballroom checking out the space. They had made a last minute decision to hire a live band, they would use a DJ for the dance. The room did not have a stage, the band would have to be off to the side a bit. The photographer Susan hired helped put together a running slide show of the foundation with photos from the makeover and of various kids from the hospital that Katie knew. It was all coming together. She made one last check with Jenny before heading to relax for a bit before getting ready.

Chilled from her walk home Allie relaxed in a steaming bath. Last week's snow had not amounted to much. She was just glad the next storm held off and would not be here for another two days. Emma had been having some fun with her by texting her every time the temperature went above 60 back in Virginia. She laughed though as they were getting hit with flurries at the very moment. Even though the cold winter was not her favorite season she would not trade living in the city for anything. Yes that was the reason she had abstained from sex. And now with Sean she could make up for that all she wanted. She let her mind drift back to St. Kitts and having breakfast in bed and champagne in bed and many other things in bed that gave her great pleasure. She had researched him well and he did the same for her. Her heated thoughts and the heat of the tub were making her woozy. Afraid of falling asleep she decided to get out. She would plan on having Sean put out her inner flames later that evening.

Back in her office Allie tossed her wool coat off and checked her hair in the mirror. The wind had been whipping hard so she opted to take a cab instead of the subway. Her hair was mostly in place, she shook out the soft curls she had created earlier. She managed to keep her dress from wrinkling as well. She chose a royal blue gown that gently swayed around her feet. The front being halter style was conservative, however the back plunged low. She loved dressing up for events and this was no exception. She hoped she chose the right mix of elegant, not overly sexy. It was black tie after all, she wanted to be taken seriously and still dress for the occasion. In any case she was happy with the way she looked. The guests would be arriving in an hour, she spun around watching the dress swish around her silver heels. She then headed to the ballroom to meet up with the rest of the team to finalize one last time the order of the evening.

The room was simple yet elegant. Black was the main color with subtle infusions of gold and purple. She was amazed at how quickly everything was coming together. And even more amazed at how she headed up a fantastic group of people that were all quickly becoming good friends to her. She had looked around and noted that the activity of last minute set up was winding down. Seeing the podium she was thinking about her speech when Kelsey came bounding in the room. She looked perfectly appropriate for a teenager and did not show her 'I'm a model side.'

"Allie, thank you so much for asking me to be here."

She wrapped her arms around Kelsey. "You are a big part of this whole foundation even happening. How is Gracie doing? I am sorry she was not able to make it."

"She is actually better. She is back at home. Her parents did not want to be too far away from her doctors right now."

"I am glad to hear that. I guess we will have to do this again, just for her. She was our inspiration after all."

"Absolutely, she will be excited."

Allie stepped back and twirled the teenager around. "You look beautiful as always."

"Thanks, you look pretty hot yourself," Kelsey said with a wink.

"Not too much?" she asked softly.

"I don't know, who's eye are you trying to catch?" she asked with one lifted eyebrow.

Well that was a loaded question Allie thought to herself, and one she was not going to contemplate. This night was not about her or James or Sean. Although James was the one supporting her tonight. He was the one stepping out of his comfort zone to help the kids. Sean said he would try to come. That was all he could promise. He did agree to take the photos at the last event but has not shown much support since. And that generally was okay with her, it just would have been nice to have him by her side as her date at least. Well it was still early. She turned back to Kelsey still looking at her with a sly eye.

"I am dressed for myself this evening," she said spinning her own self around this time.

"We will see about that," she replied as she skipped away to talk to Cheryl.

Allie watched her go and smiled. Things were more black and white when you were young, the older you got the more shades of gray that complicated life. And at that moment a striking figure wearing a very flattering grey with a slight sheen suit entered the room. Allie's heart skipped a beat at the sight of him. He looked liked he should be the model and not the agent. His dark hair was freshly trimmed and slicked back. His dark eyes managed to shine bright. Allie continued to watch him as he scanned the room, he seemed more relaxed. And confident, and sure of himself, which made him even more attractive. She wondered what the change was. She was about to go talk to him when a tall stunning woman with long black hair wearing an equally stunning red dress entered the room. Of course she was James' date. Why should she expect anything less of him she thought as she watched James wrap his arm around the woman's waist.

She could not help but watch them, he smiled and gave her a soft kiss on the cheek. Allies was not sure what to feel, then James finally saw her and their eyes locked. She looked away first unsure what he was thinking. It was as if his confidence wavered for just that moment. She shivered from that one look then shook it off. She was happy for him. Happy for herself, she had a boyfriend and now he had a date. That settled the matter, James was moving on. Not with her though. Of course not, she had a boyfriend she kept reminded herself. She put those thoughts aside. Straightening her shoulders and putting on her hostess smile she walked over to greet her friend. Yes, that was it, her friend.

"Hi, James, you look good." She had not planned on any physical contact but he pulled her to him in a friendly embrace, or so she thought.

The kiss he gave her on the cheek was friendly. The soft touch on her lower back sent shivers up her bare spine. The warm breath on her neck as he whispered you are stunning in her ear almost made her sway in her heels.

She quickly pulled away though and noticed the same look burning right through her, still could not read those dark eyes especially not with super hot date standing a few inches away. Allie quickly pulled back without further comment or glance. "I am Allie," she offered her hand,

"Selena," the dark hair woman answered with a warm smile.

"From the art gallery?" Allie asked thinking the woman looked familiar.

"Yes that is right. James told me about the charity. It is a wonderful thing you are doing. I have donated some of my dresses for your winter ball and anything else you need, please ask."

"Thank you so much, please enjoy yourself tonight." Of course she would be nice Allie thought. She did not know if it would be better to hate his date or be happy that he hooked up with someone nice. Be happy for your friend, keep repeating that thought. She went back to hostess mode and started welcoming guests.

Her excitement level jumped when she saw Molly and Jason come in the room. It had been a while since she had seen her friends. She went and gave them warm hugs, "thank you for coming."

"We would not have missed this for anything. Talk about moving here and making things happen!"

Allie jumped in not wanting to take all of the credit, "I don't think I could have done this without your moms help Jason."

"I am just glad she has something to focus on other than wondering when we will give her grand babies."

They all laughed then Molly asked, "is my sister causing you any trouble?"

Allie knew she was referring to her little ghost that sometimes shows up in her apartment where Molly lived before her.

"As a matter of fact I believe we had a little disagreement over my choice of dress for this evening. I had tried on an elegant but slightly less revealing dress last night. I am sure I hung it carefully back on the the hanger. Well this morning it was in a heap on the floor." Allie watched as Molly's eyes widened, though more in humor than in surprise. "That is not all, I decided to hang it near the shower, let the steam get the wrinkles out. Everything was fine when I got out. When I went back to hang my towel somehow it was back on the floor, now with wet spots."

"Oh no, I am sorry, I hope it is not ruined," Molly said with genuine concern.

"No it will be fine, I just was not sure if this one was too much."

"I would have to agree with Julie, it is perfect."

"Molly, I owe you so much."

"No," she said back quickly, "you are giving back. I don't need anything. Go on and work your magic tonight so you can help the kids. That is repayment enough."

Feeling blessed Allie let her friends find seats at the dinner tables. With an extra boost of confidence she continued greeting the steady stream of supporters.

Once the majority of the guests had arrived Allie took the podium and welcomed everyone. She talked about how the foundation got started and the goal of making every child feel good about themselves. She introduced her wonderful group of friends that helped put the event together acknowledging each one as she said their name. When she introduced James she could not look at him long. One quick glance and she saw his bright eyes and slight smile, she almost lost her momentum. Yet she had to give him the most credit. "And James has been with me on this the entire time. Without having met him we all would not be here tonight. So thank you James for being by my side even when you were not sure." This time she put on her genuine smile and set off a round of applause.

James felt like the kid in school that did not want the extra attention from the teacher. Except this particular teacher had a smile that always warmed him. She came to this city with goals and by some random chance that smile found him. And that smile gets him every time. And so he did what was needed and gave her a slight nod and looked away. Still feeling slightly embarrassed he shoved his hands in his pockets and scanned the crowd. He found his date. Cheryl had urged him to call Selena. He wavered all week despite his decision to put himself back out there, easy to say harder to do. He had worried about his decision to let Cheryl pick a date for him. In the end Cheryl somehow knew what he needed. Selena was fantastic, beautiful, knew her art and was successful. He knew her in her modeling days and supported her through the start of her art career and she was by his side through his darkest days. Eventually he freaked out when she seemed to be getting too close to him. He asked her to back off and she did. She was totally understanding and at the time he failed to recognize what that meant. As with everyone else he held her at arms length. When they did come across each other it was back to being good friends. No hard feelings. That is why he called her and maybe to see if there was still something between them, to see if he could put himself out there.

He heard Allie introduce Kelsey and he turned his focus back to the podium. Allie was still beaming as she gave the brave girl a hug. He was proud of both the ladies standing there and he knew at that moment he made the right decision. Allie's heart was one he would never play with. She walked over to stand next to him and he gave her hand a little squeeze. He whispered in her ear, "you were great." He felt some of the nervous tension leave as took a deep breath.

He stayed where he was and focused on Kelsey trying to keep the image of the royal blue gown pushed aside. He was proud of Kelsey, she had poise and grace that was beyond her teenage years. You had to be careful with teen models, either they did well or went crazy ending up with the wrong crowd. Of course her parents kept a fairly tight rein on her, not a bad thing for now. He was pretty confident she would remain grounded when she reached legal adulthood.

James glanced around the room realizing he was not paying much attention to what Kelsey was saying. Everyone else was though as they held their attention to her. He looked back over as she showed pictures of her friend Gracie and some of the other kids from the makeover event. She wrapped up her speech by saying every kid and every person is beautiful in their own way and deserves the chance to feel beautiful. There was a huge round of applause which made Kelsey blush slightly. She held a huge grin as she stepped aside.

That was James' signal to take the podium. Public speaking was not his favorite thing to do and he planned on keeping it short and sweet. "Thank you Kelsey, that was a beautiful speech. Thank you everyone for coming, of course any donation will be greatly appreciated. We are hosting a winter ball for a group of special kids. My assistant Cheryl will be taking dress and formal wear donations. And one last thank you to Allie for kicking my butt into gear and putting my resources to good use." He turned towards her and started another round of applause. She smiled at him, another one of those heart warming smiles. He held on to her gaze for as long as he could.

The applause let up so he turned away and when he did he saw that at some point Sean had entered the room. He knew that expression, the one that said you are treading on my territory. The same one he would have used himself. He quickly stepped aside. He found Selena and beelined towards her, his safety net. He let her give him a hug. It was comforting and it was like coming home. Unfortunately, he suddenly realized that it stopped there. He did not know why, she was beautiful, successful and amazing and why his feelings did not go further he could not understand. Maybe he never had allowed himself. Maybe subconsciously he would not allow himself to lose his safety net. They stepped away from each other and James grabbed her hand and gave her an appreciative smile. Rubbing the back of her hand he decided it was time to let go of safe, he would give Selena more of a chance. Feeling content as Selena squeezed his hand back, he did notice a slightly suspicious look on her face. "Thanks for coming tonight."

"You know I am always here for you."

"I am sorry I have not called much lately."

"You never have to apologize to me, you know that. Besides it is great to see you involved with such a special charity and an amazing group of people."

"Um, yeah," he managed to stammer out as he guided his date to two empty chairs. Technically he should have been at the table with Allie and the others. It was just getting too awkward with Sean around. Pulling the chair out for his date he managed to get his thoughts back together. "Everyone has been great. We could not have done so much in such a short time without all the help."

He sat down and poured the wine the hotel donated into the glasses. He almost choked on it when her heard Selena.

"You like her don't you?"

Not this again he thought to himself. "Of course, she is a good friend." He actually managed to take a larger swig of the wine this time. "And she has a boyfriend," he added pointing his glass to the pair.

"Why are we sitting over here then and not with the group?"

James shrugged the comment off, "letting them have their private time."

"Whatever you say lover boy."

James put his glass down a little more heavily that he planned. Wanting to show her he made his decision he tuned towards her. Taking her head in both his hands he leaned in and softly placed his lips on hers. It was just enough to let her know it was more than a kiss between friends, that there would be more to come. He caressed her cheeks with his thumb before pulling back. It was a nice kiss, not fireworks, good enough to make him want to try for more. "That is what I have to say about that," was his verbal response.

Allie wished James and Selena had sat at her table. As one of the organizers it was his right to be there. She was sure James was avoiding Sean. She felt the tension as soon as she saw him and she was sure James noticed it as well. Boys were possessive and territorial. She was tired of feeling like she has to choose between them. And really she had already made her decision. Sean was her boyfriend and James would remain her friend.

And it looked like James had made his own decision. She saw the kiss between James and his date. Happy for him, that was what she was. She took another swig of her own wine and turned back to her date. Maybe it was better to keep the distance between them. Not that there was any issue being with Sean. That was definitely not a problem. Sean looked great in his linen suit. She ran her hand across his thigh looking forward to taking off that suit later on.

She could feel him respond to her touch and she gave him a mischievous grin. She stood up pulling him with her. "Let's start the dancing."

"Absolutely," he answered while giving her his own taste of what would come later that evening before leading her to the dance floor. Once they started dancing more people joined them. The band played a great mix of fast and slow along with all the newest group dances including something called the wobble which Kelsey led. Allie laughed as she attempted to follow the steps. Sean was even goofier in his attempt, they had the electric slide down pat though. Everyone joined in; Cheryl, Susan, Katie, Jenny, Selena, Molly and Jason. Those who did not join, not surprisingly, James, whooped and hollered to keep the group going.

When dinner was called Allie made her way around the room thanking everyone for coming and reminding the guests to visit the silent auction. She was glad to see James doing the same. Occasionally she would catch his attention and give a nod of her appreciation.

Dinner service went well, Allie even managed to eat a few bites. The dessert tables were decadent with Italian cookies and pastries. Dancing continued afterwards and guests battled during the last few minutes of the auction.

At the end of the night, exhaustion was edged out by elation. The fundraiser was far more successful than Allie could have hoped. They had racks of formal dresses with more promised to come. They raised enough money to more then cover the winter ball.

Part of the hotel donating the space was having to help move the tables and chairs so the carpets could be cleaned. To her surprise Sean offered to stay and help. Once the dinnerware was cleared she kicked off her shoes and started stacking chairs. With everyone helping it only took a few minutes and she gave one last thank you for everyones hard work. She lingered with Sean as everyone said their good byes and left.

Sean took her and they twirled a few more times around the dance floor. There was no music, just two people in tune with each other. Allie let her man take the lead. Her nerves tingled as his intense eyes wandered over her body. After one last turn he dipped her backwards and followed with a kiss that declared her his. She kissed back in acceptance while letting herself fall completely in his arms. And when he growled an invitation back to his place she readily accepted.

Chapter 11

The next two weeks kept everyone busy getting ready for the ball. James and Cheryl handled the dress fittings and make up. Susan arranged the decorations and flowers. Allie and Jenny arranged the food and music. Katie kept up with the invites and responses. They held meetings, in public places as Sean requested. James was helpful and productive. Allie was a little sad that he pretty much came and left with everyone else.

She did manage a five minute conversation with him one time. He had not heard if Haley was coming to the ball, he was busy with booking runway shows and he had been out with Selena a few times. He declined a lunch invitation and said maybe after the ball they could get together. She missed her friend, the one that showed her the city's treasures, the one that made her feel not like an outsider.

She did have Sean though and he did make her happy. She enjoyed the comfort of knowing there was someone she could turn to and be with. Not that the relationship was especially progressing since Sean was also busy with the runway shows. He could not even promise he would be at the ball. Although he had become much more supportive of the charity and the extra time it occupied her. And they did manage to find a good routine of breakfast dates and spending a few weekday nights together.

The final days before the ball were even crazier for everyone. Allie was excited and running on caffeine. Her good friend and old roommate, Emma and her boyfriend Ben were coming into town. She had eagerly agreed to be the official photographer for the ball. Sure she could have found someone local, keeping her close friends involved was more important. Her brother Alex was on spring break from school and also making the trip. She had invited her mother though she rarely travelled and not surprisingly turned down the invite.

They had one last meeting the Tuesday before the ball to hammer out the final details. They had a final count, the girls outnumbered the boys but there would be enough hopefully to encourage some partner dancing. Seating would be at random which is why they decided on elegant buffet dining instead of table service. Most everything on the menu was geared to the kids and they had an amazing dessert buffet planned including a chocolate fountain and build your own sundae station.

Cheryl reported she fitted many of the girls into the donated dresses and Susan updated the group on the decor. Thanks to generous donations they were able to install a false ceiling with LED shooting stars. There would also be a wishing well under the stars and any coins tossed in would be donated back to the hospitals. With everything in place the only thing left to do was to shop for a new dress for herself.

Allie had taken the day off from work the day of the ball. She was at the hotel as all were on deck to set up to keep costs down. The only thing they outsourced was the installation of the ceiling. James borrowed a truck to pick up flowers, table and chair covers. Susan brought in additional twinkle lights and Jenny kept up with the kitchen staff tweaking the menus.

As the decor was coming together she felt a tap on her shoulder. When she turned she nearly shrieked with delight. "Emma," she gave her friend a huge bear hug.

"I am so excited to be back," she said when Allie finally let her go. Emma had been the photographer for Molly and Jason's wedding.

"Thanks for agreeing to come. How are you guys? How is business and the bed and breakfast?" Allie was anxious to hear everything.

Emma laughed, "things are going well, we should be up and running in about two months."

"That's fantastic. Ben," she looked over, "taking good care of Emma?" She once threatened him if he did not.

"Always and forever," he winked at her then gave Emma a soft kiss on the lips.

Allie was so glad to see her friend happy and full of joy, she had endured such heartbreak prior to meeting Ben.

"You must come and stay with us when we open," Allie heard Emma say.

"You know I will."

"And don't forget about me," a deeper voice said from behind them. It was Alex coming in with Katie.

Allie clapped her hands all giddy, "all my favorite people are here." She gave her brother and Katie quick welcoming hugs. Those two were another couple she often wondered at and was slightly jealous of. Even though they played the long distance game every time she saw them together it was as if they saw each other every day yet seemed more in love every day as well. She reminded herself as she still felt excited to see Sean and was looking forward to him being her date for the night. Although he may not be there the whole night, he did finally promise to get there. Either way she had all of her close friends with her and not much could make the night go bad.

Once she had guests settled into their rooms at the hotel she went to her office to get herself ready. She took an extra long extra hot shower in the staff bathroom. After brushing most of her hair into a high bun she dried and curled the few wisps of hair she let frame each side of her face. A light application of makeup and tear drop earrings were put in before stepping into her dress. She had chosen an ivory colored strapless gown. The bodice was fitted and embellished with crystals and flowed out to a small train behind her. She thought it was elegant without being too showy and it fitted the winter theme. She put one final spritz in her hair, took a deep breath and headed to the ball room.

James was pacing the ballroom, he had help set up the DJ stand and now there was not much left to do. He had changed into his tux so he was just waiting. Selena would be arriving a little later and he had a dance promised to a special teenage girl. He hoped she would be there and was unsure of her health status. He was still getting used to the idea of seeing the kids in various stages of treatment. He knew this would be a special night and all his anxiety was nothing compared to what the kids went through on a daily basis.

He was trying to pay attention to Cheryl as she rambled on about who had chosen which dress and could not wait to see them all made up. He shook hands and made small talk with Alex and Ben as they all had ladies they were waiting on. Still with the small distractions he was unable to shake his anxiousness.

And then she came in the room. Allie, as always, was able to calm his nerves just by being present. He smiled as she approached. He wondered if this is what a groom felt like awaiting his bride when they finally opened the closed doors hiding his prize. The whole world went away and it was only the happy couple, nothing else mattered. As she came towards the men he finally noticed the gown that somehow did not wash out her light skin and golden hair but made her radiate even more.

He knew she acknowledged his smile when he saw her eyes drop quickly to the floor and then look away. What he did not expect was for her to approach the other men first. Of course one was her brother and he should expect that but it felt like a mild insult. Which he deserved. He had kept his distance the last few weeks. He needed the step back, he needed his own space to test the relationship waters with Selena. They had been out a few times and he enjoyed her company. He took her to his bed on the last date and they both were physically satisfied. It was a good start for him and he did want to be distracted from any possible feelings for Allie. She had her relationship and he had his own and that is where he intended to keep things.

"You look handsome," Allie said bringing him back to the moment. She gave him a quick hug and squeeze of the hand. "Are you ready for this?"

His hand tingled from her touch yet it still calmed him. "I am, thank you," he said sincerely knowing she would know what he meant. She was the reason he was slowly coming out of his feeling sorry for himself funk and getting him back out and putting his skills to use.

She did not verbally respond, just held his gaze for a moment. Then she turned to address everyone, "here we go," she said with enthusiasm, "I am going to head out to the lobby and greet our special guests."

Allie was still feeling her natural high from the adrenalin and excitement. She felt good with James as if a silent understanding had just passed between them. She felt more certain they could develop a level of friendship that would not interfere with each others relationships. They would never likely double date or sit down at a restaurant together but getting back to discovering the best street food she was sure they would do. And she was content with that. And they still had the foundation together.

She had yet to stop smiling and when she saw Kelsey coming towards her and she smiled even bigger. She looked beautiful in her aqua colored dress that swept the floor. With a simple sweetheart neckline and spaghetti straps she was glad to see she was dressing her age, her modeling kept her looking too mature as it was.

"Gorgeous dress, it brings out your green eyes," Allie told her.

"Thanks, I love yours too. You look like a bride."

Allie had considered that when she tried on the gown, only for a moment though. "It's winter white," she replied with a smile.

"Hey are going to dance with James tonight?" she asked as swirled through the lobby.

"I don't know," Allie answered honestly. "I guess I will have to see if he asks me."

Kelsey rolled her eyes, "you don't have to be so old fashioned you know. You could ask him yourself."

"Hmm, I am not so sure about that. Go get ready to do the flowers okay?"

She shrugged her shoulders and skipped over to her station. Susan had been able to get another generous donation of wrist corsages and boutonnieres. Kelsey wanted to be the one to hand them out. Cheryl was with her as she set up a temporary coat rack. Katie was at the table with the name place cards. While there was no table numbers she thought they would make a nice scrapbook souvenir and guests could then hold places at tables if they wished. Jenny, James and Susan would be greeting guests inside the ballroom and Emma was already roaming taking photos.

The first guest arrived marking the official start of the Shooting Star Wishes Winter Ball. And with any event that you spend so much time planning, time seemed to suddenly speed up. Within twenty minutes most of the guests had arrived. Cheryl, Jenny and Katie agreed to take shifts in the lobby. Kelsey left to talk to the kids and Allie followed behind. She did stay back just enough to allow the doors to the room close. She wanted to make a quiet entrance, steal a moment to take in the decor, the guests and the overall atmosphere. She slowly pushed open one of the double doors and stepped to the side. The lights to the room had been dimmed, the shooting star ceiling was breathtaking. The twinkle lights strung around the rest of the room resembled a city skyline. There were glittering snowflakes hanging throughout the space. They still used the deep purple with minimal gold accents which tied the whole room together. The wishing well was lined in LED rope lights with chasing bulbs giving it a more modern look that would appeal to the kids. And the kids looked amazing. Even if some of them looked a little uncomfortable in their formal wear the portraits Emma would take would be priceless to the parents.

It was probably less then a minute that she stood there but it was a moment she would cherish for a long time. She was proud of herself and everyone involved. And now it was time to get the party started. Susan and James were greeting and directing guests though there seemed to be an uncertainty as to what to do next. Allie scanned the room and found Kelsey.

"The kids are going to follow your lead, why don't you take some of them to get food then we sill start the dancing once a few more kids arrive."

"I can do that," she said heading over to a small group. Kelsey was turning into a wonderful host. She was turning into a wonderful young lady and hoped she would have a lasting relationship with her.

In the meantime Allie made her way around the room, introducing herself and talking with parents. She did not plan on any announcements or speeches, she wanted to keep the evening more personal and intimate. The kids were starting to separate from their parents which made it easier for Allie to make her rounds. Many of the parents were taking their own photos while letting the kids mill around on their own. Allie noted some of them tearing up especially when they thanked her for putting on the event. Allie knew that might happen and she vowed to keep her own emotions in check. No matter what was going on with each kid here she knew she was giving them a special memory.

Once a few more guests filtered in and most everyone had eaten a plate of food Allie once again turned to Kelsey. She grabbed her hand and they headed to the wishing well. Allie had left a few coins nearby for those who did not have any. She grabbed one, waited to see a shooting star pass over head then closed her eyes and threw it in.

Kelsey did the same, "no telling otherwise it won't come true."

"It is all right, I think all of my dreams of being here have come true." And she truly meant it.

"Are you sure about that?" Kelsey asked with a quizzical look.

"I am sure, now go on and get the dancing started, ask the DJ to play something upbeat."

"Okay, don't forget your dance with James," she said with a wink before running off.

Allie also went around the room grabbing people and hauling them to the dance floor. The boys were a little harder though. With some of the quieter ones she actually asked them to dance herself. She would do a few waltz steps with them then get funky just to get them laughing. Honestly she was not a great dancer herself, she did not care what she looked like and neither should the kids. As she made fun of herself the kids became more relaxed and willing to let themselves go. Of course there were a few show off kids doing hip hop and breakdancing. The whole room joined in clapping and cheering.

When dance floor was full Allie stepped aside to take a breather. A glint of light caught her eye. It was the double doors opening. A frail girl was being brought in. She was struggling to sit up in her wheelchair yet she had enough energy to form a smile when she fully entered the room. Starting to head over to greet them Allie stopped when James got to her first. She realized she was the one he talked to at the makeover. While she had not participated then she was glad to see she had come in a gown. Even though it hung a bit on her body it almost brought tears to Allie's eyes knowing that all this was truly for this one beautiful girl. She hoped James could handle seeing her so frail. She would give them time and then talk to him. That she would do as his friend.

James admitted to himself that he was enjoying the evening. Talking to the parents put his anxiety about the kids at ease, they just wanted to have a normal day and an opportunity to have fun with others that understood. He encouraged kids to dance as well but kept his own self off the dance floor. Mostly he hung around the wishing well. It was a good spot for him to get used to talking freely to the kids, some wanted to tell their wishes and others did not. And for those that did it gave him a sense of pride being the keeper of their deepest wishes. Surprisingly only a few wished for better health, most wanted normal things that other kids wanted as well: to be asked out, a new video game, to learn to drive.

And then his own heart almost stopped. At first he was not sure that was Haley being pushed through the door. When he saw her smile though he knew it was her. He hated that he was scared, scared for her and of her. Luckily his feet took over and walked him to her, surely she was the scared one as she was so frail and her skin was pale. As he approached he slowed his breathing and got control of his emotions. This was not about him, this was about making her final wish come true.

He greeted her parents, they had dark circles under their eyes and they looked weary. "Thank you for coming," he said.

"She insisted," her mother commented, "we can't stay long though."

"I understand," he said then squatted down next to Haley.

"You look stunning," he said softly picking up her hand to kiss the back of it. "I was afraid you were going to stand me up," he added to lighten the mood, mostly for himself.

"I never promised to be your date," she said, a slight blush coming to her cheeks. "Where is your date?"

James pushed his hair back and looked down, "she is not here yet."

Haley stretched up a bit looking around then looked back at James, "isn't that her; the one in the ivory dress and blond hair?"

"Um, well we are the hosts of the event. I have another date, she is not here yet though." James barely stammered out the words. Wanting a distraction he stood up and addressed her parents, "mind if I take her to the wishing well?"

"Go ahead," they nodded.

"Please have a seat and enjoy some food, I promise to take good care of her." The couple looked at each other and holding hands walked over to the buffet.

When they reached the well Haley obligingly took the coin from James but only twirled it in her hand. James had squatted down next to her again. She looked at him kindly, "you know I don't have time for any more wishes."

James heart was breaking, of course he knew that as soon as he saw her, it did not make it any easier to hear it from her though. It was not fair that her life would end so soon. His anger flared up, it was not fair his child's life never got started.

Sensing something was wrong Haley went ahead and threw in the coin, "you don't have to worry about me, I am not scared."

"You are way braver then you should be," he told her squashing his anger with a deep sigh, it was time to get past it. Then remembering something she had told him he asked her, "did Julie come to visit you?"

This time she had the slight look of embarrassment, "she came a while ago, before we met."

"You already knew?"

She shrugged, "she told me I needed to go to your makeover and talk to you. Seemed kind of strange at the time."

James closed his eyes in a moment of debate and decided to say it anyway. "Julie sometimes visits Allie's apartment, or so we think. That is where her sister used to live."

"Ah," she said with more glint to her eyes then should be there, "makes total sense now."

"Oh it does, does it?" he asked playing dumb.

"You know James, I told you already. Take it from me, life is way too short to ignore the things you want."

James took both of Haley's hands in his and rubbed her palms. "I know," he said, and he did but for now he wanted something else. "Would you honor me with a dance?"

She tried to pull her hands away, he would not let her though. "I don't think I can," she whispered.

"Hold on," he told her. He ran over to the DJ and made a song request. He pushed Haley's wheelchair into the middle of the dance floor. When the song 'Somewhere Over the Rainbow' started he lifted her up and placed her arms around his neck. "Put your feet on mine," he told her.

He held one arm around her waist with the other supporting her upper back. He softly placed her head on his shoulder. He did not need to know how to dance, he just took small steps around the dance floor. Most everyone else had stopped dancing. He did not care that everyone was watching. He knew he had just granted a young lady her last wish. He focused on holding his partner and the lyrics of the song which he whispered to Haley. He was glad they played the longer version and yet he wished it could keep going.

When it ended he knew it was time to let Haley sit back down, her breathing was slightly more labored from the effort of holding on. He was worried what she would look like, again he needed to stop with that. Despite her dwindling energy she had a huge smile on her face. His heart leapt, there was no other moment he could compare to this.

"Now you owe me a promise," she said in between breaths. She nodded towards the woman she made him promise to be there with.

He stood up, one dance, he could manage that.

Allie saw him come towards her. She was not sure she breathed during that whole dance. The whole room was quiet and watching. She quickly wiped the tear that threatened to roll down her cheek. She noted others were doing the same. Turning her attention back to him, his eyes were intensely watching her. She could not decipher the look. It could have been pure desire or let's get this over with.

"Shall we?" he asked with his outstretched hand.

"Of course," she said taking it. Of course she would in front of all those people. They knew who the hosts were and to decline would be inappropriate. She followed him to the center of the floor. Haley was still parked there and she was still smiling. Allie winked at her before turning to face James. She was not sure if she felt lucky or unlucky when 'Halo' came on, another slow song. It was something they could both manage but it meant they had to stand close to one another.

And as they began to take a few tentative steps they pulled a little closer to each other. She was not sure if it was her doing or his. At that moment she did not care, she relaxed into him, they fit a little too perfectly. With her heels she was tall enough to comfortably rest her chin on his shoulder. She felt him entwine his fingers through hers while holding her close with the other hand on the small of her back. Her whole body was tingling from her fingers through her spine and right down to her toes. She closed her eyes ignoring the audience. She was a bit relieved when Susan and her husband joined them leading a bunch of couples onto the floor as well.

When the song ended James gently pushed her back and twirled her around. He bowed with a sly smile and went back to Haley. Allie watched as he pushed her off the dance floor. Her head was swimming with all the emotions surrounding the night. She needed a cool drink.

She headed to the buffet table and had another mixed jolt of emotions. Sean was loading a plate with food. Actually she was happy to see him. Her date finally arrived. She gently put a hand on his back so she would not startle him causing food to go flying everywhere. "Hey handsome," she said softly in his ear.

Sean turned to her and took a appreciative glance at her, "hey beautiful," he said before kissing her lightly.

Allie was hoping for a slightly more enthusiastic greeting as she watched him focus back on the food. "Long day?"

"Yeah, I am actually kind of worn out," he told her as they headed to some empty seats.

"I truly appreciate you coming." Allie tucked her foot around his and made some small talk about the night so that he could eat. Afterwards they took a few twirls around the dance floor. Sean was quite a good dancer, not only did he lead Allie around he was able to entertain some of the kids as well.

Allie noted that Selena had arrived at some point also. She and James seemed to be having a good time as well though she tried not to pay too much attention to them. Selena did get James out on the dance floor one more time and they all sort of nodded at each other in passing.

Once the dessert tables were rolled out Sean indicated he was ready to head out. "I will walk you out," Allie told him grabbing his hand.

In the lobby she turned and hugged him lingering with her head on his shoulder. "Maybe I can come to your place tonight. It might be pretty late but I don't mind."

Sean stepped back and looked at the floor, "I don't know, I am pretty tired and I have another full day tomorrow."

"Okay." She took his hands and pulled them towards her lips and kissed each one. She was happy when he closed his eyes, she knew she was getting to him. "I am off tomorrow night," she was still enticing him.

"I have no idea what time I will be done."

Allie pulled him in and pressed her lips against his, she wrapped her arms around his back and he took the bait, kissing her deeper in return. When they came up for air she told him with no uncertainty, "either way we are doing Sunday breakfast in bed."

His only acknowledgement was another soft kiss and squeeze of the hand. She watched him go and when he reached to door, he turned, "you were amazing tonight."

She smiled back, happy for the acknowledgment that she had been waiting from him.

The rest of the evening went well. The dessert selections were a big hit though possibly a little mess for formal wear. They would have to think about that the next time. After that some went back to dancing, others starting to trickle out. It was another round of thank you, hugs and handshakes. Even Selena acknowledged her and promised a donation.

After the last guests had left Allie changed out of her dress as it was clean up time. The whole group stayed to clear the tables and stack the chairs. The lights were taken down, the ceiling would be removed the next morning. With everyone helping it was fast work.

Several people were actually staying at the hotel that night, Allie was not sure why she had not thought of that herself. She was tired and it would be easy to crash for the night but her own bed was calling her. After saying her thanks and goodnights to everyone she went to her office to change and pack up.

When she came out James was still hanging around. She was thankful when he spoke first, at this point she was not sure what to say to him. All the thanks had been spoken.

"Sean leave?" he asked straight to the point.

"Yes, he had a long day."

"Hmm," he grunted shuffling around.

Allie just stared at him and when he said no more she started heading to the door.

"He should be taking you home," he said just as she was about to reach for the door handle.

Allie turned back around starting to feel a little defensive, "he was tired. It's no big deal. I can get myself home, I do this everyday."

James eyes darkened as he pinched his eyebrows together. "He was your date he should have escorted you home."

Allie sighed, she was tired, "what about you? I don't see your date here."

"That's different, she did not need to stay for the clean up. And she lives much closer."

"And neither did Sean," she was starting to get angry. "I am not having this argument with you James." She turned and yanked the door open. A blast of very cold air hit her and the door almost closed shut before she made it out. She started to walk to the subway station when a hand on her shoulder made her turn. Seeing James did not slow her pace down.

"Then I will take you home," James told her as he caught up.

"Um, no I don't think so," hell no was more like it she thought silently to herself. She shrugged her shoulder to get his hand off her.

Luckily James knew when to back off. "At least let me get you a cab."

She knew when to give in. She turned, "fine, it is really cold out here anyway."

Chapter 12

All the adrenalin of the past week wore off in one swoop. As soon as her head hit the pillow she was out cold. What seemed like five minutes later she was woken up by a pounding. She was not sure if it was her head or construction work nearby. She managed to lift one heavy eyelid to realize it was light out. She looked at her clock, not quite time to get up. Her head thumped back down on the pillow. The pounding would not stop, then she realized it was partly her head from lack of sleep and mostly someone knocking at her door.

She groaned and rolled over, maybe if she ignored it they would go away. Finally she got up as she realized whoever was there probably knew she was home. With another deep sigh she threw the covers off. She grabbed her robe from the hook on the inside of the bathroom door. She had not bothered with pajamas last night, she had thrown her clothes off and left them in a heap on the floor before climbing into bed. She did not bother to look at herself in the mirror, she already knew it would not be good. Shuffling towards the door she at least shook out her hair.

Allie peeked though the little hole in the door and almost went back to bed. She was not in a mood to talk to

James. They were having such a nice night, she did not know why he had to get on her about Sean. Even his own date had left early. Her friendship with him was getting too difficult, she was having trouble finding a happy medium with him. Maybe it was not possible to have male friends while in a relationship. No, she did not believe that. She decided to let him in even though she knew there was a good chance it may shatter their friendship.

Allie unlocked the door and slid the chain over. She opened the door and gestured for James to come in without speaking. She watched as he walked in rubbing the coldness out of his hands. She did not think it was just cold air, dark circles under his eyes portrayed the real cause of his pale complexion. While she had slept deeply out of exhaustion, it appeared he did not sleep last night. He was also fidgeting; rubbing his eyes, running his hands though his hair, smoothing down his coat. Normally he was more laid back, she was back to wishing she had stayed in bed. She was not in the mood to play counselor this morning for whatever was going on with him.

She did let him in though so she at least needed to be cordial and wait for him to let out whatever he needed to say. She added water and beans to the coffee pot and switched it on. While it was percolating Allie washed out a pair of coffee mugs. She was purposely keeping her back to James. She could still hear him shuffling around. Finally she heard the scrapping of a chair indicating he was sitting at the table.

With nothing left to do, she had no food left to make breakfast, she grabbed the mugs and turned to set them on the table. Only when she turned James was right behind her instead of sitting at the table. Time slowed as she felt herself being pushed backwards into the counter, the mugs were taken from her hands. Despite having appeared cold the weight of James' body pressing into her instantly spread an intense heat though her core. When she looked up dark eyes were shifting though a huge range of emotions. Loneliness, longing, desire mixed in with a little fear.

Allie was frozen, hands gripping the counter behind her. She could not help but to tilt her head back as James cradled his hands on either cheek. She knew she should turn away, stop him. His lips were soft, gentle, caring. She was losing the battle to stand, the tingle went all the way down to her toes. Strong arms moved around to her back supporting her melting body.

Just as James pushed harder with his kiss a mug crashed to the floor startling both of them. Allie jumped slightly and pulled back. Slightly confused as to why Julie, assuming it was her again, would interrupt them, Allie was more concerned as James seemed to be coming back for more.

She pressed her hands against his chest, "James," she barely managed to say above a whisper, "please don't."

The look of pain in his eyes almost tore her apart. She started to feel a twinge of hurt in her own heart. Why was timing always so off with them? "Please, I can't do this right now, this is not fair."

James, head held low, was quiet as he twirled his finger through Allie's hair. "Haley passed away early this morning," he told her without looking up

"I'm sorry," she said with genuine concern and sadness. Although they had expected it it was still heartbreaking. She took his hand in hers. "You gave her the best night ever, I don't think there was a dry eye in the room when you danced with her."

"Dancing with you brought the smile to her face, that is what I will remember."

"James," Allie started.

"No, please let me finish. Since we met you have been the only light keeping me going. I had crawled in a dark hole and then came you, this woman just trying to make me laugh. I was a fool for keeping you at arms length. And now, this trying to just be friends thing." James inched a little closer, "I can't do this anymore. I can't fight my feelings for you."

Allie literally felt her heart squeezing and her breathing was coming in short rapid bursts. She was getting annoyed that he was doing this now, he had been pulling away from her for the last month. She had gotten used to the fact that his role in her life was changing. Sean had been her focus, along with the foundation, of course. Still she had reconciled with James' decision to step back even if it was partly Sean who had forced it. And here she was again having to choose between a solid relationship she was building or risking her heart with someone that she feared may still not quite be ready for a commitment. And was she really supposed to suddenly break up with Sean just because James changed his mind?

Allie pushed him away, anger replacing the tingling. "This is not fair. I gave you multiple opportunities, made my feelings clear to you then respected you, yet stood by you all this time. So now I am supposed to drop Sean because now you changed your mind?" Allie's anger was dissipating as she noticed the hurt in James' eyes. Still, what was she supposed to do? She let her eyes drop to the floor and bit her tongue. Her hands were starting to shake but she would not allow the tears to come. Not now, not yet. Especially when she had a feeling this would be a no win situation for her. Her first friendship since she had moved to the city was dissolving.

"I know I am being selfish," she heard James say softly. And when he tried to take another step back towards her Allie shook her head. He stopped and shoved his hands in his pockets. "I did not sleep last night. I am a mess, I went in and out my door so many times this morning. Now, seeing you, I can't believe how foolish I have been. I am sorry it took me all this time. I'm sorry I let Sean push us apart. I would say I am sorry for asking you to take a chance on me except I am not."

He wanted to reach out to her again, reassure her and feel her soft hair and silky skin and never let her go. Yes, he was being selfish and yes he was going to be even be more unfair. If he left without an answer she would go see Sean and he might just convince her to stay with him. That thought taunted him the whole ride, almost made him turn back. And if she did make that decision it would be his own foolish fault. And the worst thing would be the loss of her friendship. Even if she wanted it he would not be able to be around her always thinking about what could have been. Even in a group setting he did not think he would be able to do it. Which was also putting the structure of the foundation on the line. Financially he would always support it, he stopped mid thought and pushed his hair back. He needed to stop thinking about being rejected and fight for what he wanted. Unfortunately communication was not his best quality. Yet he knew Allie and he knew she understood him and what it took for him to be there.

Allie squeezed her eyes shut, she struggled to take normal breaths. She was still confused, unsure of her own emotions and there was a trust issue. Finally she looked straight into James eyes, "how do I know you won't get cold feet again? If I let go of Sean, how do I really know you won't break my heart in a few weeks or few months?"

James knew it would come down to this, he was the one all along saying he was not ready. The only thing he could do now was be honest. "I know it would be foolish to make a promise, I just know how I feel about you. You made me smile again and you helped me do something meaningful. I hated seeing you with Sean, but I think you knew that," he added with a sly smile. When she did not show any reaction he started to feel more unsure then he had ever been in his life. "Please Allie, I don't want to lose you."

Allie was feeling dizzy with emotions and more likely from her erratic breathing. A part of her just wanted to jump in his arms and a lot her could not get past this sudden turn around. "I need time to think about this." And space she thought to herself.

James had a look of complete defeat, He grabbed Allie's hand and just rubbed it. "I was really hoping you would at least give me a chance," he told her quietly.

She pulled away partly in frustration, "if you are expecting an answer right now, I can't do that. You know that is not fair."

"I guess I thought it would be an easier choice between Sean and me. I guess I underestimated him." He turned and quickly headed to the door. "I am sorry Allie, I screwed up, I will leave you alone."

And before she could answer he left. She stared at the closed door until another coffee mug hit the floor. She bent to the floor to pick up the broken ceramic, little Julie did not seem to like her decision. Allie was not sure if she liked her decision. She stayed there hands over her eyes, tears running down her face.

"And so he left, just like that?" Emma asked her friend.

Allie, Emma and Ben were siting in the small greek diner near Allie's apartment. It was the same one where Molly and Jason met again before becoming engaged. The restaurant was small but always busy and the food was good. Allie wanted to show her friends some sites around the city. Of course Ben used to live there but Emma wanted to play tourist. They all had been there together the year before for Molly's wedding and it was good to be back. Emma had her camera and wanted to see some of the more unusual sites. She wanted to start with the park where she photographed some special pre wedding photos. Even though Allie felt it was still bare and grey she knew Emma had a special eye that created amazing photos.

And while she was trying her best to enjoy the day James' visit had her emotions in a knot. And it was not just James, she knew the kids that came to their events were sick, not all of them would recover. Still it was a tough reality and she needed to think of some way to pay respects to the family from the foundation. Symbolic stars in the name of the kids to make wishes on. The first one for Haley. She would have to come back to that. She wished she could ignore her earlier meeting and get back to that later also. That would not happen with her best friends sitting with her. "I don't understand how he expected me to decide right then and there."

"He probably spent a long time working up the courage," Ben said between inhaling his eggs and hash browns.

Allie closed her eyes and sighed, "and I shot him down." Allie noted the sympathetic faces from her friends. Still she did not think he was being fair and yet she realized her friends did not seem to agree. "Are you taking his side?"

"No, just making sure you are making the right decision."

"I don't know what that is."

"Are you sure?" Emma asked with a firmer tone. "When we talk you tell me about what you and James are doing, you very rarely mention Sean. If you love Sean that is fine I just am not sure that you do."

"Things are good with Sean," Allie said defensively.

"Good?" Ben asked. "What about great, fantastic?"

"Do you see a future with him?" Emma added.

"I don't think good is really good enough," Ben said

Allie's head was spinning with the questions. They were hard questions, ones she had been ignoring. "I do not know. I at least owe a visit to Sean."

Which Allie was not able to do that day. Luckily she was able to at least try to enjoy her company. Her brother and his girlfriend joined them. They spent the day touring iconic sites including the World Trade Center memorial. After the somber visit they continued on their be a tourist day by going to the top of the Empire State Building. By the time they were outside taking in the views the sun was starting to dip towards the horizon. Alex gathered the group to watch and after a moment turned and got down on one knee in front of Katie. There was a collective gasp from the group when they saw the small box presumably holding a diamond ring.

"Katie, we met by chance and you took a chance on me. And it has not been easy doing the long distance relationship. I am two months from graduating and can not wait to spend a lifetime with you in this great city. And if you will be my wife you will make me the happiest man alive."

Katie's hand was shaking as she nodded yes. "Are you sure you can handle my crazy family?" she asked. "Because they come with the package."

Alex stood up laughing, his new fiancé had some pretty protective brothers and he knew there would be a threat not to break her heart, part in good fun part in all seriousness. They were a great family and he would be thrilled to be a part of it. "I can handle it, including your brothers. Plus with Allie here I will feel like I am home."

There were hugs and high fives and tears of joy. Although Allie was glad she could hide her tears as joy. She was truly happy for her brother and she loved Katie as well and looked forward to having her as a sister in law. Yet she wanted to know why it seemed so easy for Alex and Katie. Was it supposed to be that easy? Emma and Ben had bumps in their journey. But now it seemed just as easy for them as well. Friendship with James was easy. She was not sure it would it would remain that way if she took a chance with him. Sean was easy in some ways. They had fun together and he was finally supporting her with the foundation. But was it better then good, could she see herself moving in with him, spending a lifetime with him? She needed to go see him.

Chapter 13

Allie barely managed a shower before heading over to Sean's place. She was beyond tired. She had been out with her brother and friends celebrating the newly engaged couple. Plus the fact she had tossed and turned all night trying to decide what to do. As she approached his building she was hoping it would feel like home, being in his apartment and back in his arms. If she felt that then the decision would be made, things would go on as they had. She was fairly convinced that her good was in fact good enough.

Allie had not told Sean she was coming by. She figured he would be home. Sunday was their usual hangout morning anyway. As she knocked on the door she realized that a small step forward would be to exchange keys. She was willing to take the step and started to get excited

Until she heard a female voice coming from just the other side of the door. She was suddenly confused and truly hoped he had a house guest that he failed to mention. And then the door opened and her heart sank. Selena stood at the door in one of Sean's robes.

"Who is it?"

Allie heard Sean's voice. Her brain froze, luckily her legs took over and carried her through the threshold into the room that she should be lounging in with her boyfriend. Her boyfriend, not Selena's. Now she was feeling anger rise, her space was being invaded, she was losing the power to make her own choice.

"Hey Allie," Sean said casually.

Which angered Allie even more. He greeted her as if she was just a friend stopping by. "What the hell is going on Sean?" she yelled at him.

"Calm down Allie," Sean retorted with his arms stuffed in his robe pockets.

"Don't you dare say that to me. How the hell am I supposed to act when I find out my boyfriend is with another woman. And one I know to boot," she pointed accusingly at Selena who was now in the kitchen making coffee. And not only that she seemed to know where everything was. "How long has this been going on? I thought you," she turned to to the woman, "hooked up with James." Her inner flame was burning hotter. They were both being cheated on.

"It's not like that." He tried to step towards her but the warning look in her eyes kept him in place.

"Bullshit, tell me how long this has been going on!"

"We hooked up after the ball. Look, I told you I did not want to be your second choice."

"And I told you," but she stopped when he threw his hand up.

"You can say all you want, however I have never been your first choice. Just because James was too damn wrapped up in his own sorrows to realize you were the best thing that ever happened to him does not mean he was never not a choice."

Allie's anger was starting to diminish. She walked over to his couch and flopped heavily in the deep cushions. Of all the scenarios she came up with prior to coming here, this was not one of them. Sean sat down next to her and he leaned into her. He wrapped his arm around her. Allie realized that it was good but not great, not home. Feeling even more deflated she also realized she had in some ways been using Sean. Yes she liked him, what she liked even more was the distraction he provided. Not that she should have sat and waited on James, not in a city full of single men. And knowing the history the two men in her life had with each other maybe she had not made the best decision to date Sean. She sat up and forced herself to look at Sean. "I am sorry," she said softly.

Sean shifted to face her, "don't be. We had a great time together."

She nodded in agreement.

"Go be with him," Sean said giving her a final hug.

Allie was still unsure though and she figured she was not being fair but decided to ask anyway. "Do you think he is ready Sean? He kept telling me he swore off women."

Sean laughed for a moment. "First let me say men can not live without women. And I don't mean having relationships. It is just not possible for us to be without female interaction for that long."

Allie rolled her eyes and jabbed him in the side.

"Seriously, I have known James for some time. I have never seen him happier with anyone else. I see the way he looks at you. You got him to do things I never imagined." Sean paused and ran his fingers through his sandy blond hair. "We have loosely or foolishly competed over women, and I will lose this one too. But it will be the last one I lose," he smiled at her, "You are the one for him. I can't promise you he will be the easiest person to live with but he will treat you well. And if he doesn't, well you know where to find me."

"Thanks. I think I have screwed this whole thing up though," Allie said as she walked to the door.

Sean followed her out. "Not even possible."

"So you like her?" Allie asked realizing that crossing back over the threshold made her officially an ex girlfriend. She knew she would eventually be okay with that. She also knew she would run into him from time to time. And she wanted to be okay with that also.

"I do like her," he said with a sincerity she knew to be true.

"Then maybe you did win after all," she said before walking away.

Allie did not go to James that day. Besides needing to go to work she still needed to think about her decision. Also a part of her was hoping he would reach out to her again, not just give up after one try. Was he willing to fight for her, if not did she want to be with that person?

She kept to herself mostly during her shift. Allie was grateful Jenny had not said much to her, she was not in the mood for lectures. She focused on menial work. She double checked schedules, spring wedding season was right around the corner and they would be even busier than the holiday season. Which was good, something to focus on. And she did have something to look forward to, she made Emma promise she could be the first guest at her and Ben's new bed and breakfast. They were almost done with the renovations and would be opening soon.

And there was her brother's wedding and graduation and she was excited he was moving to the city as well. And spring was coming which meant new leaves, new flowers and warmer weather. She was pretty sure James was no longer in the picture. She did not want to chase him down, she had given him multiple opportunities. Maybe she was being foolish, maybe the fight had been drained out of her.

It was towards the end of the night and things were quiet all around. Allie was doodling on some paper drawing flowers and wedding dress designs. She was doing it without thinking. When she snapped back to reality with the knocking at her door she tore the sheet of paper off her pad and threw it in the garbage.

She looked at her clock, there was only a few minutes before she could go home. Whoever it was better make it quick. "Come in."

"Hey," Jenny said as she cautiously approached her boss. Allie had made it clear when she came to work she did not want to talk about "it". And she had just recently found out what "it" was. And while she hated to disturb her at the end of her shift she really had no choice.

"What's up?" Allie asked looking very tired.

"There are a few complaints of noise coming from the roof."

Allie contemplated that for a moment. They were in the process of constructing a rooftop lounge slated to open late spring. There should not have been any construction going on at the moment. "Is the rooftop access door locked? The contractor is supposed to do that at the end of the day." And it was Sunday, there should not have been anyone up there anyway.

"Oh I am not sure. Come on I will go with you."

Allie gave her a look of suspicion. Still she could not ignore the possibility there was a problem. She grabbed her pass keys and jacket and followed her assistant out the door.

They left the office and passed through the quiet lobby on the way to the elevators. Allie used her key card to gain access to the top floor where the large executive suites were located. They followed the hallway to the end where the stairwell was located and passed through another door to the roof top stairwell. Eventually a new entrance would be constructed for hotel guests. Allie had to punch in a pass code to keep the alarm from going off. Which made her doubt there was much more going on other then some wind blowing around some construction debris.

When she pushed the heavy door open she was greeted by a blast of cold air that immediately turned her cheeks red. She threw her wool coat on before stepping outside. She turned to make sure Jenny was coming then noticed she had not brought her blazer. Not wanting her friend to freeze she told her to wait there, "if I don't come back in two minutes come find me."

"Okay," Jenny agreed a little too quickly for Allie's comfort.

Another one of her stupid decisions Allie thought to herself as she took a cautious step out on to the roof. Even though the air was cold there was a stillness that Allie was grateful for. She was also grateful the wall marking the lounge area was already built, not that she was afraid of heights, it just gave her more confidence walking around.

As her eyes adjusted to the moonlit night she did not notice anything in particular or out of the ordinary. She walked a few feet and did a quick scan of the area. She decided she would walk a little further and peek around the bar area that was under construction. Then she would either call her boss or decide it was an unfounded complaint. In any case it could be checked out the next morning and she could say she at least attempted to see what was going on.

As she walked up to the new bar she noticed a faint glow coming from around the other side. She was not sure if it was light from the adjoining building or someone with a flashlight. Her heart started beating a little faster and she looked around for something she could pick up as a weapon. Not that she knew how to fight or even wanted to. Unfortunately for her the construction crew was meticulous, which was good in its own way, though it meant there was nothing she could find to grab in a pinch. She decided to hold still for a moment and listen. All seemed to be quiet other than the street noise coming from below and the low light did not move which would indicate it was not a flashlight.

Heart still pounding she had enough. Turning to head back she jumped when she heard the access door open. She had not realized the first time how much noise it made. She expected to see Jenny instead a dark figure came through. Frozen in place she felt trapped and stupid for coming out by herself. Then she had a serious panic moment when she wondered what happened to Jenny. Her panic quickly turned into anger and right back to fear. A combination of fear and exhaustion caused a few hot tears to start running down her frozen face.

While her brain was still processing the situation she thought she heard a voice calling her name. A random cold breeze whipped around her forcing her back to self preservation mode. It was time to figure out how to get back to safety. She was gearing up to make a push past the stranger and sprint down the stairs.

"Allie," she heard again.

Only this time, as her brain was functioning again, she recognized the voice. Allie took a closer look to make sure she was right. And to her great relief she was. James stood there in his long wool coat. The moon reflected in his dark eyes adding to the shadowy figure effect. Allie was trembling and now to add to the range of emotions she already was experiencing, confusion was now coming to the top. "James?" she called out in a shaking voice.

"It's me, I am sorry. We thought this was would be better then you finding me up here already."

"We? What is gong on?"

James quickly crossed the space between them and grabbed Allie's hand. "Come with me."

A part of her wanted to pull away and make him explain first. Wanting to get back in the warm air enticed her to follow him. She would give him a minute then find some other much warmer place to talk. And if she was honest with herself she was not sure she was in the mood. The only comfort was the warmth coming from James' hand. It was sending a tingling up her arm that she was trying to ignore. Adding anymore emotions to the evening was not what she wanted.

And sometimes it did not matter what the practical side of her wanted. As they turned the corner the warmth spread through the rest of her with a surge she could not tamper down. Part of it was truly physical with the heat lamps surrounding the pergola. The teak wood was wrapped in twinkle lights which was also contributing to the soft glow she saw just a few moments earlier. Under the pergola was a queen size chaise lounge draped in multiple layers of quilts and fluffed up pillows.

James finally stopped in front of the lounger and turned Allie towards him. He too was a mess of nerves. After she had rejected him the morning before he was ready to crawl back in his hole and not come out. He knew had not been fair asking her to make a decision on the spot. A part of him thought it would be cut and dry. They had been on the edge of flirting their entire relationship. And yes he was a fool for pushing her away. After Haley had convinced him to live the life he wanted he spent the night convincing himself she would just run into his arms. When she did not it was a blow to his state of emotions. He had finally decided to open his heart back up and the woman he knew he loved hesitated.

So he ran. And he almost kept running until he got back to his apartment and his coffee mug was on the floor in pieces. He was positive he had not knocked it over before he left and there was no way someone had come into his apartment just to break a mug. He had sat on the floor staring at the broken pieces for a long time equating them to the mess he had made of his life. Then he realized it was Allie that had glued him back together. And it was a special teenager that could point out what was plainly clear. Now he was ready to fight, fight for his heart and his future happiness. He did not even want to imagine how he would feel if this did not work.

He did not feel the cold, his heart racing, his nerves on edge, being so close to Allie all kept him warm. Allie on the other hand appeared to be shaking, he knew partly from nerves also. He took her hands in his and rubbed the cold out of them. Then he brought them closer to his lips and when she did not resist he gently kissed her soft hands. He felt her start to relax. Now was the time to him to make his case.

James let go of one her hands and pressed his palm against her red cheek. "Allie, I am sorry about yesterday, I should not have pressured you, especially considering your current relationship." James paused to take a deep breath. Sean was a decent guy, he inwardly cringed every time he saw them together. "I am in love with you and we belong together. You brought me back to life. And we work well together, created an amazing foundation. I want to keep building it with you and I want to keep finding food treasures with you and travel more with you and mostly I just want to see your beautiful self everyday. So here I am asking you to be with me. I know it is not fair to ask you to end things with Sean, I," he was going to keep going when he felt Allie's fingers on his lips.

Allie could let him ramble on, she would not mind hearing him say he loved her all night long. She also knew how hard this was for him. "Sean and I are no longer."

"Okay," he said slowly, he could not think of any real appropriate way to react.

"Selena and Sean hooked up Friday night, she answered his door in his robe this morning."

"Well shit, now I really don't know what to say," he did pull her closer and held her head against his shoulder.

Allie let him comfort her, she admitted it felt good and it felt right being in his arms. She was not feeling too bad about Sean. "It is all right, he saw through me. I did try to make it work though."

"Do you want me to go punch him in the face for you?"

Allie half laughed at the vengeful look on his face, his already dark eyes managed to become a shade even darker. "No, it's fine."

"No it's not, that was wrong. I don't care what Selena does, hell we were never an official anything. What Sean did was wrong. He should have broke it off with you first."

She needed to calm him down quickly. "Forget about it please," she pleaded with him. "They actually seem to like each other."

"Still does not make it right."

"I know, now can we get back to you telling me how much you like me," she pleaded with a seductive smile on her face.

"Like is the not the right word," he whispered in her ear, "I am fully in love with you." He went to lean in for a kiss, the first kiss they could truly share without restraint.

Allie knew he was coming yet she still needed to make absolutely sure. She pulled back and watched his head drop in frustration. She took his head in her hands and made him look at her. "Promise me you are ready for this, that you won't be scared and run away in a week or a month. I don't think I can take losing you again," she whispered since her voice was starting to tremble.

James held onto her as tight as he could and breathed in the sweet coconut scent of her hair. He knew the only thing he could do was speak honestly from his heart. This was a new experience for him. Allie made him want to be open and honest. "I can't promise I will be perfect, I can't promise

I will be the easiest person to be with. I can't even promise I won't have moments of doubt. What I can promise you is to tell you when I do and I give you permission to knock me back to reality, throw a coffee cup at me." He could tell she was hiding a grin. "Allie, I don't plan on letting you go," he said with earnest.

"Oh James, I am in love with you too." This time she went in first and dove into a kiss that instantly made the cold go away. She felt his hands wrap around her back and through her hair. She leaned further into his warm body and plunged deeper into the kiss. Her inner core was starting to burn and she needed to suck in a gulp of cold air. She pulled back and looked at her man's face. She liked that, her man. He was breathing just as hard as she was. She smiled at him then looked at the chaise lounge. "So what do you have planned for this evening?" she asked taking her coat off and tossing it to the side.

After doing the same he grabbed her around the waist and toppled her onto the cushion of blankets. "I plan on making up for months of dreaming about you," he said in a low husky voice.

"And you think I am going to be that easy?" she teased him while sliding her hands under his shirt. His skin was smooth and warm and she could feel his muscles rippling with her touch.

"I don't think you will ever be easy," he said with a gleam in his eye. "I do know you want me." He reached down for another brief kiss. He pulled away again and sat up. "You can tell me to stop anytime you want."

"As if I could," she reached up to him and ran her hands up his shirt and pulled it over his head. She started kissing him just under his ear down the side of his neck and across his shoulder. She could hear him letting out soft moans causing her body to react in ways she has never felt. Thoroughly enjoying the reaction she was getting out of him she continued across his chest until she found his nipples where she circled her tongue around each one. His groans were getting deeper, he grabbed her shoulders pulling at her blouse. She kept going further down past his navel reaching the top of his slacks. His body tensed under her, smiling she sat up and rubbed her hands across his pecks and further down where she unbuttoned and unzipped his pants. There was a pulsing bulge waiting to be released. Allie reached back and yanked off his leather dress shoes then slid his slacks down past his ankles and onto the floor.

Which gave James a chance to reposition himself. He was hot and ready for more and wanted her to keep going. He wanted to taste her more though. He sat up and held her in his lap. Only her skirt was in the way, He disposed of that quickly along with her heels. Next he unbuttoned her blouse slowly, one button at a time while kissing her jaw and neck. She leaned back some to give him full access which he took full advantage of. After the last button was freed he reached behind her and popped her bra free as well. James pushed the silk down her arms followed with the bra straps. He was slowly exposing her taking in her beautiful creamy skin and her rounded breasts.

Undressed to his satisfaction he rolled her onto her back and pulled the blankets over them. "So beautiful," he told her taking in her sight and doing nothing else.

Allie's body was quivering with need. "I need you to touch me James."

"Oh I will, patience my lovely creature."

Allie moaned in response and reached down take off James' last remaining garment. She threw her leg across him pretending to pin him down to her while she stroked his hardness with her hand. He was pulsing with desire just as urgent as hers but he would not let her continue.

James easily pulled back from her grip and pinned her hands above her head. "Not yet I said." He let go of her arms trusting that she would behave. He cupped her breast in his hand stroking her nipple to attention then took it into his mouth for more tasting and teasing, He gave each one equal attention. When Allie wrapped her legs around his back pushing her hips up into his he finally gave her what she was pleading for. He stretched out next to her and took her swollen lips back into his. He wrapped an arm over top of her so he could rub his hand across her forehead. With his free hand he trailed his fingers down her chin and chest circling around each breast then stopping atop her panties just as she did to him. He tugged at the lace garment and pulled them down to her thighs. He trailed softly back up her thighs one side at a time hesitating just short of her sweet spot. He wasn't purposely torturing her, he was enjoying her squirm. He would not be mean though so he ran his fingers through her soft curls and immediately noticed her moisture ready to guide him in. She pressed into his touch which heightened his own desire, he did not even know he could desire a person this much. And it was more than desire, it was a deep love, a wanting to pleasure this woman more then he cared about himself. He pressed into her alternating between her inner and outer sweet spots. He pulled away from her lips as her breathing became rapid. He went back to tasting her breasts, heightening her desire. She pushed against him harder moaning and digging her hands into his head pulling at his hair.

He increased his pace responding to her until her whole body tensed. She quivered and let her hips drop back down. He was ready to burst himself, he pulled her panties off the rest of the way and quickly found one of his condoms and slid it on. He thought Allie was still in recovery mode. To his surprise she was still fully alert and in another quick second had him rolled on his back. She straddled him slowly lowering herself to his burning rage. Teasing him back she let him just feel the tip of her wetness. With an evil grin she circled around him without letting him in. With a deep growl he grabbed her hips and pushed up towards her.

Allie gave in and let him in a few centimeters at a time. He filled her entirely and wanted to adjust to him and savor the moment. When he was fully in her she slowly rocked back and forth. She watched his face, eyes closed deep in concentration which she was about to break. She adjusted her angle and pushed in deeper. His eyes flew open and an animalistic groan escaped him. Feeling her own desire start to come back she picked up the pace. He rocked with her lifting her higher trying to push deeper into her. She knew a second climax was coming, she tightening around him and pushed harder, she could feel his release which sent a pulse into her and with one last thrust came for the second time. She slowed to a bare minimum teasing out the last pulses of desire for both of them. She collapsed on top of him letting him stay inside of her a moment longer.

James savored the moment briefly, he knew the cold air would quickly chill his sweet beautiful woman. Yes she was his, he pulled the blankets back over her shoulders as he let her slide off him. She stretched out to his side while keeping her arm and leg thrown across him. He rolled into her pulling her tight into his body. Kissing her nose and lips and eyelids, he said, "I am definitely never letting you go."

Allie sighed in complete contentment. She turned and looked up at the sky. It was a clear night, there were more stars out then she thought would be possible. The longer she looked the more pinpoints of light she noticed. Then it happened, the moment made just for them, a star shot across the sky. "Did you see that?" Allie asked James with quiet excitement.

"Make a wish," he said appropriately

"I don't think I need to," Allie snuggled back around the warmth next to her.

"Did your wish come true, the one you made on the beach?"

"I think you know the answer to that."

They were standing on soft white sand, a soft breeze was blowing. It did not do much to cool the warm air though. Allie looked at the still waters of the bay. There were egrets fishing, blue herons flying across the deep blue cloudless sky. The sun was setting casting a hint of pink across the sky. It was absolutely perfect. She turned her attention back to the couple standing under the pergola. She smiled when she heard Katie say I do to her new husband, Allie's brother. Having no sisters Katie had asked her to be one of the bridesmaids which she gladly accepted. James was the best man. She snuck a glance at him, he looked incredibly delicious in his linen pants and flowing white shirt, they contrasted nicely against his sun darkened skin and dark hair.

She knew the newly married couple was happy and excited. All of their friends and family made the trip to the newly opened bed and breakfast Allie's mother had even made the trip from the Martha's Vineyard estate she took care of. Katie's brothers and parents also made the trip from New York. As did Molly and Jason as maid of honor and groomsman. Even though Kelsey was technically too old she still made a beautiful flower girl. The whole crew was back together for a weekend wedding celebration.

As promised Allie was the first guest at the new Back Bay Bed and Breakfast. They had driven down from the city two days prior to help with the final set up. Ben and Emma had worked hard to get the place renovated for the summer season. They were giving Allie and James a tour of the property. There was a waterfront restaurant that would serve guests breakfast then open for lunch and dinner. The marina had been rebuilt to allow boaters to stop by for a meal. The marina also had jet skis and kayaks for guest use. New sand had been brought onto the beach, a few private cabanas were built facing the water of the bay. The guest house was in the old beach style fashion with shingled siding, a broad porch with ceiling fans and rockers completing the touch.

A small lap pool with attached spa glistened behind the main house surrounded by vegetable gardens that served the restaurant. The rooms were each decorated slightly differently in hues of cream, soft blues, greens and yellows reflecting the surrounding nature. The walls were adorned with Emma's photographs she had taken on her various kayaking tours she guided.

As they walked the halls Emma's mother was skittering about making sure every detail was in place. "Don't mind her," Emma said. "She has been a little OCD getting ready for the the opening."

Allie laughed, "no worries, she will make a great manager here." It was a perfect position for the divorced woman who was a housewife and community activist most of her life.

"This place is amazing," James told the couple. "You did a great job."

"We are almost booked up for the summer season," Emma said beaming with pride."Here is the key to your room," Emma handed over the key card. "See you in the morning," she said with a wink.

Allie looked down to take the card and noticed the twinkle of diamond surrounded by white gold and smaller diamonds on Emma's left ring finger. She picked up her friend's hand with the card and looked closer at the antique ring. "What is this?" she asked accusingly as she had not been notified.

"We got married last weekend," Emma said matter of fact.

"What? And you did not tell me!" Then Allie remembered the glow of pride on Emma's face, "Are you pregnant?" she asked with a half shriek.

Emma shook her head in affirmation. "We just want to keep it quiet until after the ceremony. We don't want to take away from your brother's day."

"But what about you guys, I can't believe you did not tell me, I would have come."

Ben jumped in, "Our ceremony was perfect, it was on a river cruise with a boat captain and now we get to party with all of our friends."

Emma noticed her friend was still a little disappointed. "We invested everything we had into this place and my mom paid for our little ceremony. Besides you will be here when the little one is born. Right?" she aded with emphasis.

"You could not keep me away," she told her best friend. They all hugged. Allie and James turned to enter their room while Emma and Ben retreated to their top floor apartment.

Once inside Allie took a moment to reflect on how lucky she was. She had a job she loved, friends she loved, a foundation that was thriving and the man she loved. She had moved in with James shortly after the night on the hotel rooftop. She had given him a house gift: a box full of I Love NY mugs. They had not broken one yet.

About the Author

Writing is about creating worlds we can jump into, worlds that provide a momentary break from our lives. The characters I create are like able and often frustrating. They will make us laugh and cry and hopefully cheer for them. Creating these worlds has provided my own personal breaks from my busy life, My full time job is as a Licensed Veterinary Technician. I am also a wife and mother to two teenage daughters, My own collection of animals included cats, dogs, a bunny, fish and three horses. We are heavily involved in The United States Pony Club and travel throughout Virginia, North Carolina and Kentucky for competitions. Traveling is another passion with Disney World being my home away from home.

Printed in the United States
By Bookmasters